Poirot and the Crown Jewels

and other stories

as told by his friend Nigel G. Hastings

by

Allen Whitlock

*For Judy*

# Contents

# CHAPTER ONE

## POIROT AND THE CONTEST

I had been called away from town for a few days, and on my return, I found Poirot in the act of strapping up his small valise. This was no small undertaking for a King penguin, or a penguin of any type for that matter, although his size proffered some advantage over smaller species.

My offers of assistance went unheeded, but I continued to nag because I'd noticed a train ticket on the entry table when I'd arrived. Poirot had little time to make it to the station when one considered his waddling gate, planting one foot forward before turning his torso in the opposite direction to land the next step.

"Your train, Poirot," I said as I took my watch from my waistcoat and sprung open the gold cover with a cheap dramatic flourish to emphasize the point.

"Our train, Hastings," Poirot stated. Then he clicked the valise's buckle into place and uttered a deep *squawk*. I knew from our years together that sound represented an expression of great satisfaction.

I went to the entry hall table, and indeed, moving the ticket on top revealed a second under it.

I told Poirot I'd rather not go, attempting to mollify him by reminding him how I feel about contests. The contest in question was, of course, the British version of the Famous Nathan's hotdog eating contest, affectionately called *Britgluxet*, which was to be held in Leicestershire this year. My objection to attending was on two counts: first, the idea of seeing contestants virtually inhale hot dogs in quantity was disgusting—I suppose I didn't have or need a second reason.

An unvoiced third objection was that Poirot was a penguin. As a creature who could slide any number of large fish into his gullet as fast as the law of gravity would allow, it was, in my opinion, not in the spirit of the contest. But I knew my friend would be hurt if I refused to accompany him, so I agreed to go.

Ever since *The Voicing*, as they now called implanting vocal abilities in animals along with verbal enhancements and amygdala damping to reduce ferocity, ethical dilemmas have presented themselves daily. The result (after twenty years now?) was that the spectacle quickly superseded any fairmindedness. Media ratings ruled. Who wouldn't want to watch American football with a rhinoceros defensive line or a Bears offense with real bears? Soon, official all-human, NFL-sanctioned games had been swept into the same bin as 1900s bicycle racing after the invention of the motor car.

Ours would be a day trip, and Poirot had all he needed in his valise and no suitcases necessary; a happy circumstance for me because he couldn't shoulder his own luggage, having no shoulders. He did have a cleverly made harness that held his *talk button* on the front of his chest. It wasn't an actual button, but the name stuck from the device's origins.

It had started innocently enough. Dog owners began to place talk buttons on the floor. When the dogs used their paws to push a button, they were able to convey their needs with recorded messages like *outside*, *treat*, *skritchies*, and other requests. Owners soon added dozens of buttons and were surprised by how many words their pets seemed to understand, as well as how many words they would use to express themselves.

Using fMRI scans, researchers could see when a dog formed an image of a ball or food bowl in their imaginations. The next step was to cause a matching pre-recorded word, say, *ball* or *food*, to kick off along with the mental image. This was a more direct means of speech than whacking a plastic device with a paw. That worked as expected for physical objects, but using A.I., patterns of emotional thoughts emerged. One day, when A.I. interpreted the brain waves of a lab assistant's Beagle named Darwin to voice, *I love you, Kera*, it opened the floodgates of both tears and commercialization.

Although small compared to human brains, dogs, cats, and, yes, penguins hid a sophisticated intelligence, simply waiting for a means to give it expression. My friend Poirot—and I'm not ashamed to call him that—was always eager to share his opinions on any matter, although he was prone to digress into dissertations concerning cold-water fish.

The story of how we met had become something of a legend within the new field of human/animal relations and was subject to the typical distortions such tales spawn. It was not, as he claimed when he led me to safety when I was lost in snow-blind conditions in Antarctica. First of all, I have never been to Antarctica, and secondly, neither has Poirot. We met on a train platform. He had wandered off from his owners—who had purchased him from a *penguin puppy mill*—the formal-looking animals, once voice-equipped, became trendy as drinks servers at parties and as butlers. His owners envisaged Poirot as a fourth for bridge; however, cards and flippers proved incompatible, so he was relegated to serving Damson gin whenever the family matriarch rang a little bell. Depressed, Poirot left one day, thinking he could make his way in the wide world with his new-found oration skills. Even now, talking penguins are rarities. However, street-corner tirades about *the low quality of mackerel these days* did little to add coins to the proverbial hat. He next tried what he referred to as tap dancing, which looked spectacular in a cartoon he'd seen but only caused passersby to ask if the pavement was hot or if he needed a vet.

I hoisted Poirot's valise, and we just made it to our train platform in time: next stop, Leicestershire, and the European version of the Nathan's Hotdog eating contest.

When we arrived, the registration queue was devoid of humans except for one person—a woman so small I thought the elephant behind her could have picked her up with his trunk and gulped her down with no more effort than one of the famous hot dogs would require. Poirot insisted on me keeping our place while he waddled down the line to check out the competition. Heads swiveled as news of a second human made its way among the contestants, and various types and sizes of eyes gawked at me. I lowered my head and stared at my shoes. I felt a bump, turned, and found that a Mountain gorilla had joined the line. Next to him was an exquisitely dressed and coifed woman about sixty years old. She was rail-thin, and I wondered how she didn't fall over due to the ornate jewelry she wore. Her gorilla also wore earrings, bracelets, plus a diamond-studded, white gold tiara on its peaked skull. The woman—who I later learned was the famously eccentric Duchess, Lady Gladwell Falswell-Whitheral of the Kent Whitherals—left the line before I could politely introduce myself, but the gorilla remained.

I had already turned in that direction and felt I needed to say something. Dull eyes under a heavy brow ridge met my gaze. I noted its button on a harness at heart level, but there seemed something odd about it; it had no brand name, and nothing lit up. I blurted some greeting—*hello, how are you*, or some such—only to get a snort in return, accompanied by a damp spray that hit me in the face. I dared not wipe it off until I turned away. I waited until I turned away to produce my pocket square to dab my face. *Where was Poirot*, I wondered. Although he'd be little protection from the ape, at least I could stop holding his place and get away for a refreshment.

When Poirot returned, he was in fine spirits, lifting his beak up and down and attempting that clumsy footwork he felt passed for dancing. He expressed that his victory would be a sure thing and that I should engage in a wager. Then, he asked if he could borrow a twenty to make a wager of his own. I declined on both counts. It was a good thing because joining the end of the line was another woman, this one nearly as large as my gorilla friend, who carried around her shoulders what was easily the largest Boa constrictor I'd ever seen. Truth be told, it was the only Boa constrictor I'd ever seen. To be even more honest, it could have been an Anaconda; I don't know one monstrous snake from another. The important part is that it was as big around as Poirot, and, calling up my limited knowledge from documentaries, I knew that it could open its jaws and swallow a dozen Poirots or, to the point, consume a world's record number of Nathan's Hot dogs.

I had no idea that reptiles were allowed, but this was a firm argument for banning them. Poirot's slim chances were now anorexic.

With Poirot back in line, I excused myself and joined the onlookers. The event was crowded, and I'd lost my chance of finding a good seat and was relegated to an overflow of late-arrivers having to watch on monitors. Twenty minutes later, raucous music signaled the beginning of the event. A gravelly-voiced announcer introduced himself as a former P.A. (Pre-Animal) World

Wrestling Champion. The monitor camera panned to the twenty or so contestants seated, standing, or draped (in the case of the snake, which I learned from its introduction was indeed a Boa constrictor named MacCrusher (apparently of some Scottish constrictor clan) behind a long table. When Poirot was introduced, he jumped up to stand on his chair, holding one flipper to his ear and waving the other as if to encourage the crowd. The gesture received a disappointing response, and he sat down in a sulk. The gorilla, next, beat its chest and bellowed. I felt this was gratuitous pandering, but the crowd went wild. More stereotypical displays followed: the elephant trumpeting, trunk raised, the Wildebeest banging its horns on the table, nearly breaking it. The sloth raised its claw when introduced, although the gesture was still incomplete when the announcer moved on to the giraffe. And so it went down the line.

All went quiet for a moment. Then, at an airhorn blast, human attendants rolled in carts. These attendants wore white jumpsuits bearing hotdog-colored vertical stripes—a color scheme that struck me as a potential safety issue considering some of the contenders' potential ferocity and reach. They set platters stacked high with hot dogs in buns in front of each contestant. The announcer started his countdown at ten, and the crowd counted along. It was deafening. At two minus a split second, all Hades broke loose. The camera fell to the floor, and my view on the monitor became a scramble of feet, hooves, and paws. Somehow, despite being at a distance of at least a hundred feet away, a hotdog and bun, still intact, hit the person next to me in the forehead. "Bloody hell!" they swore, brushing their face frantically as if they walked into a spider web.

As one is instructed to get out of a riptide, I went sideways through the escaping mob and found myself in an overgrown grassy area. From there, I was able to see the stage. My friend, Poirot, had hopped up on one of the tables, kicking aside buns and hot dogs and gesticulating wildly at the chaos around him. The five or six attendants in their colorful outfits who'd been bringing out hotdog platters were fleeing, dodging creatures, or diving off the front of the stage into the crowd like musicians at a punk rock concert. Sadly, this audience lacked the organization of your typical mosh pit—the attendants who'd chosen that better part of valor landed on the grass with a thud.

Most of the twenty animal contestants quickly made their way off the back of the stage, following the elephant who cleared a path through the tables and audio equipment. Only the sloth, who was still holding his first hotdog, remained. In the midst of this, the gorilla was in a fierce battle with the Boa constrictor, who'd wrapped itself twice around the gorilla's torso, its head halfway inside the gorilla's jaws. Lady Falswell-Whitheral ran up the temporary stairs to the right side of the stage like some heroic goddess, her jewelry flashing in the stage lights. The duchess grabbed the Boa with both hands and pulled. She pulled until her gorilla ejected the snake with a mighty *GHAAK!* Poirot jumped off his table, dodging the mad duchess, the snake's whipping body, and the gorilla's flailing limbs, and rolled off the front stage where I had run to catch him, breaking his fall.

On our walk back to the train depot, I asked what I'd missed. It seemed that Lady Falswell-Whitheral's gorilla was a ringer—an unimplanted plant—a ringer she'd no doubt hoped would unleash its raw animal rage on the piles of food. Instead, seeing the Boa constrictor pulling ahead, it tried a shortcut, attempting to eat the slithery competitor—dogs and all—for the win.

We rode the train back in silence, and although it was late and traditionally the time for sherry, we each settled for a nice cuppa with lemon for me and cream for Poirot.

After a moment, I set my cup in its saucer and asked, "What did you think of the contest?"

My plump, feathered friend rubbed his belly and complained between burps and hiccups, "There was apparently no selection process—an unmodified gorilla? I put myself in mortal danger simply by being on the stage. But the worst was what they made us eat—hot dogs! Have you ever eaten one of those foul things, Hastings?"

"No, but I gather people rather like them…." I started, meaning to modify my statement to include that the venue—a sporting event or a barbeque, not to mention the addition of mustard—no doubt made all the difference, but he cut me off.

"I rather think no one—man or beast—could possibly like such a thing. Now, a mackerel—a mackerel would fit that bun nicely—that's the way to go. That's the…."

I took his cup just before he nodded off.

# CHAPTER TWO

## PENGUIN ON THE LAM

I was to meet Poirot for lunch at our usual sushi spot. After a reasonable wait of twenty minutes, I started to rise when Poirot brushed past and hopped up into the chair across from me. I pushed my chair back and stood. "What in Christ's blue heaven, P—?"

Before I could say his name, he cut me off with a squawk and a furtive flipper.

"Hastings! My name is Jerome," Poirot said in the warbling voice of a disguised witness on a true-crime show. He wore a tan raincoat and yellow tufts stuck straight out from either side of his head.

My left eyebrow attempted to escape into my hairline. "What the devil are you supposed to be?"

"Shush, Hastings. Sit, sit. Obviously, I am a Southern Rock penguin. You would have known that from my side feathers if you knew anything about the genus Euripides." He swung his head this way and that so that his attachments—more bristles cut from a broom than feathers—caught the light. "I have recently immigrated from Antarctica."

Imagining that some nutrition would be required for whatever Poirot had to tell me, I caught the waitress's attention and waved her over so we could order.

I sat back down, leaned over the table, and whispered, "I believe that the genus for crested penguins is Eudyptes. Euripides was an ancient playwright." I tapped the paper menu that lay in front of Poirot so he would be ready to order. "Secondly, the Southern Rock penguin hails from the Falkland Islands, not Antarctica," I stated this with some authority, having previously boned up a bit on penguins due to our friendship. I often sought to share information, but Poirot quickly lost interest beyond the photos.

I should have said nothing. I simply meant to point out an error in his disguise. Poirot was a product of a penguin "puppy mill." Nestlings were raised for a certain number of weeks and then sent to some unnamed former Eastern Bloc country for language chip installation. To Poirot, Antarctica is a mythological cover, like the stork, regarding where human babies come from. I didn't press. I considered how I'd feel if my life began when *unboxed* by someone who'd purchased me as a pet and pressed the *on button*. None of us want our protective delusions cruelly ripped from us. For most of us, with love, time can heal all wounds. But perhaps it wasn't so for a four-foot-high surgically enhanced bird separated from his species and familiar background, so a grounding myth was needed. That was why I never pressed him on Antarctica.

Antarctica also plays into other of Poirot's fanciful tales. For example, we did not meet one another on an ice floe in that foreboding continent but rather outside the Victoria Coach Station. He was half-starved and busking by passing off a clumsy waddle as dancing while reciting self-written poems, sounding suspiciously like those of certain Romantic period poets, primarily concerning cold water fish.

"Why the disguise?" I asked, gesturing to the protrusions on either side of his head.

"Ah, Hastings, let me show you." With that, he dug his flippers into the side pockets of his raincoat, extracting bits of torn paper. "I pulled this post down from a café pinboard."

I had to suppose that beaks and flippers were not the

ideal appendages for removing a poster intact. Smaller pieces fell to the floor until he got to a larger one that he laid out on the table. I smoothed it out and, though incomplete——I saw that it was an advertisement as one found tacked up concerning lost cats or dogs or, in this case, a penguin.

REWA… (I assume REWARD… the rest was torn away.)

Underneath was an image of a King penguin—Poirot's species—on what remained of this portion of the poster, no doubt clipped from the internet. It had been printed in color and showed the King penguin's distinctive bright orange mandible markings. I looked at Poirot. I'd failed to notice that he'd blackened his own bright orange markings—with what I shuddered to guess was likely a magic marker.

Before we met, he'd left his previous situation as butler and companion for a woman, her daughter, and son-in-law who lived in a grand house in Old Chelsea. When his flippers proved inadequate at handling cards as a fourth for bridge, his duties were reduced to answering the door and serving drinks at the matron's frequent teas or serving her Damson gin whenever, night or day, that she rang a tiny, silver-handled crystal bell. *The bell! The bell!* Poirot would tell me, holding his flippers to his ears. *It was driving me mad!* I knew how and why he had left, yet, foolishly, I did not grasp that it had been an escape.

"Where is the rest of it—the lower half?" I asked, then realized it could no doubt be assembled from the other scraps of paper that had fallen to the floor. The waitress arrived. She was perhaps forty, an attractive woman with dyed black hair accented with white streaks. Her silver nose ring, skull earrings, and Egyptian-styled eye makeup completed a look that made the amateur psychologist side of me place her as someone unwilling to let go of a rebellious past. Her work outfit was a black apron over a white shirt. I expected a snarl, but she smiled cordially. I immediately regretted my judgmental presumption.

She leaned over towards Poirot, then looked at me and asked if he was mine.

"No," I replied. "He's his own man… or penguin."

"A Southern Rock penguin," Poirot emphasized his statement by swishing his head about, displaying the bristles on the sides of his head. How he attached them to his head was a mystery to me. I feared some found adhesive—chewing gum found on the street perhaps. The bristles themselves—an artificial dayglo yellow— reminded me of the broom in our hall closet. I made a mental note to purchase a replacement broom.

"Oh, my," the waitress clucked. "You *are* a ways from home then. My hubby was in the Falklands war, poor man. Said he loved seeing your mates when he was there."

Saying we were pressed for time, I ordered our food before Poirot could start in about Antarctica. California rolls for me and the chef's selection sashimi, hira-zukuri style but with no wasabi, for Poirot. Before leaving, she bent down and picked up the pieces of paper. She started to put them in her apron pocket.

"Sorry, I need them."

She placed them on the table before me. "There you go, love."

I thanked her, and then, wishing I had some tape, I assembled the pieces, printed side up, and fitted them to the remains of the main sheet with the photo of the penguin. A fringe of cut sections at the bottom displayed a phone number; some had been taken, lost, or perhaps swallowed in Poirot's frenzied attack. There was no name or address.

*Subject lost near Old Chelsea.*
*Call if seen.*
*Answers to the name Poirot, or may respond to ringing a bell.*

I read the assembled poster aloud. The last bit about the bell got a squawk from Poirot that turned heads.

"This would be…?"

"Yes, yes, Hastings. The old bat and her wretched brood."

"Now, now, old man."

Poirot sulked, shrinking into his raincoat.

My inclination, nature, personality, or character—whichever you choose—has always been to face problems head-on. Despite the occasional knock to the old bean, I still adhere to the ideal. I settled Poirot in my apartment, making him promise to stay hidden there while I went out alone to make inquiries. This was agreeable to Poirot as his disguise was looking the worse for wear, and he'd been staying in his room for the most part. Leaving, I remembered to check the hall closet. There, I solved two mysteries. First, I confirmed that his headdress was made from bristles taken from the hall broom. Next, finding the remains of said broom now stuck to the floor next to the mangled tube of super-glue I'd kept in my office/workshop for my model airplane hobby, I discovered the means Poirot used to affix his disguise. I made a second mental note to purchase a new broom and a new tube of glue.

I first went to my solicitor. Making an appointment would have been polite of me, but when were cousins ever polite? And Averill owed me for ratting on me for smoking after school. She was only six. Still, I've held it over her ever since.

"Avy," I said as we greeted as warmly as British families greet. She did not get up when I was shown into her office. I wanted a legal opinion on Poirot's purchaser's ownership rights before contacting them. I explained Poirot's situation as she sat behind her desk, fingers appropriately bridged, reading glasses properly riding at half-mast on her aquiline nose.

With the occasional squint in her hazel eyes and pursed lips now and then, she let me string the story uninterrupted. I kept it brief, leaving out the hotdog eating contest and his penchant for extended mackerel odes.

When I'd finished, Averill sat up and slapped the blotter in front of her, startling me.

"Good lord, Limpy—a hell of a thing."

I wish she'd stop calling me that horrible nickname. It seemed I'd never live down that incident with the goat. The limp had been temporary; the damage to Aunt G's fence was still evident if you knew where to look. The goat, last I heard, was thriving.

"How so, old girl?" She wasn't old.

Averill tapped her intercom, "Westly, bring me the Rollins' file."—pause— "...and the Smithers' giraffe case. No, bring me everything involving animals. Don't bother with the pet store gerbil bite case; only cases involving enhanced animals."

Westly affirmed the request over the intercom.

"I, uh..." words threatened to fail me.

Averill sat back and looked at the ceiling. "That might have been a hamster." She looked back toward me. "No matter."

"I just wanted advice on Poirot's situation."

"What you brought me—why hadn't you mentioned it

before? Your little penguin friend could be the tip of a massive legal iceberg." She chuckled. "Iceberg."

I tried to remember if icebergs were in the Southern Atlantic or if they were only a North Atlantic phenomenon—I only had the Titanic to go on. Certainly, there were no icebergs around the Falkland Islands where King penguins such as Poirot originated. Then, I snapped my mind back to the problem I'd come to see Averill about.

"But about my friend…."

"I see a massive class action suit," she continued, "representing every one of these poor creatures—given verbal skills without their permission. The horror of self-awareness thrust upon them."

I had always thought of self-awareness as a gift or at least an aspiration—though unclaimed by the majority of humans as far as I could see. "Do you really think self-awareness is a horror?"

"Of course, it's a horror, dearest cousin. It brings the awareness of one's own demise—the crushing existential burden of impending doom. Have you not read poetry? Surely, you've read a book."

I've read several books and was tempted to list them in my defense, but I needed to get Avy back on track.

"This penguin of yours, is he photogenic? Of course, they all are. Penguins are so cute. He'll be perfect. Can we change the name? Poirot is so French."

"Poirot is a Belgian name," I said with more confidence than my knowledge merited. My friend was named by his previous owners, who were, one must assume, Agatha Christie readers. In turn, I assumed that Mrs. Christie knew what she was doing in naming her Belgian detective.

"Belgian? Even worse. We must think of a good English name. Reginald has a sort of penguiny ring to it.

It is male, yes?"

"The name is masculine." I then wondered if Poirot was certain of his gender. The name and the voice were male, but his purchasers had assigned them. Would anyone know unless he started laying eggs?

Averill made a move to pick up her phone, and I vaulted into focused action.

"Avy, stop. This is all well and good—the immediate problem is that my friend is in hiding—on the lam, as they say."

She started laughing. "You thought that goat was a lamb. Oh, your face when it lowered its head to ram you."

"I don't recall the event with near the hilarity."

"Of course not; you were the butt, as it were, of the joke." She reached for a tissue and dabbed her eyes.

"Poirot is my friend," I said, and it occurred to me how to get Avy back on track. "My friend won't be of any use to you as the spearpoint for your legal action if he's captured and given back to his owners. I doubt they'd warm to you showing up to take his deposition. Possession being—whatever that ratio is—will not be in our favor."

This seemed to sober her. I could imagine the wheels turning in her head, animating her tapping fingers, and making her eyes dart from side to side like an eighteenth-century automaton. I took this as a sign of deep and complex legal cogitation and leaned forward in my chair with expectation.

"Chicken and egg." she declared, paused, then burst out with, "No, penguin and egg!" she slapped her desk and clucked at her own witticism. "You hit upon it, Limpy—no doubt accidentally—but you hit upon the core legal issue."

"Have I?"

"Nine-tenths. Possession is nine-tenths of the law, by the way."

"So, Poirot must serve as their butler every tenth day," I said, joking. "Or," I continued, "does it mean that I own Poirot, and they must bugger off—excuse my crudity."

"Silly. If a thief breaks into your flat, steals a watch, and gets caught on the way out, do they have the law on their side because they have the watch in their grubby little hands?"

"So, the nine-tenths thing is…"

"It means the thief will likely be found guilty of possessing the stolen object. To the law, possession equates to control. The thief could claim someone slipped the watch into their pocket, but the preponderance of evidence—the ninety percent, if you will—is against him."

"Oh, that's rather backward than I dare say most people think of it."

"Most people are idiots. Which gets us back to you."

"Now, see here."

"Oh, I do. I see that you currently possess a stolen object—one Poirot, the penguin. So, if they contend he is an object stolen from them, then why haven't they pressed charges and had you arrested for keeping a stolen object? I propose we bring the matter to the police. Having you arrested would press the matter."

"I can assure you I have no interest in such an outcome."

"No, no. We should demand it. Think of stolen art. Keeping it at your flat would be considered theft. If Poirot is an object, then you have been breaking the law. If not an object, you have not been breaking the law."

"Schrödinger's felon then?"

Using the information on one of the posters, Averill contacted the aggrieved party and filed a motion. Poirot's previous owners agreed to arbitration at the plaintiff's solicitor's offices, but only if we guaranteed that Poirot would be there. Averill warned me that they expected it to be a quick judgment and that if things went badly, they'd be leaving, bird in tow.

The day of the hearing arrived. When we arrived, Mrs. Gladis Fenn, her daughter, Mrs. Alto Willowart-Nestig, and Mrs. Fenn's son-in-law, William Willowart-Nestig, were already seated at the conference table along with their solicitor, Addison Kemp. Averill motioned for me to sit next to her on the opposite side.

I should mention that I had not seen Poirot for the past several days. He had secluded himself in his room in my apartment, choosing times I was away for his meals and ablations, which was more frequent than usual because I was working with Averill on his case. I had just sat down when he entered. I assumed it was Poirot anyway—it would have been quite the coincidence if another penguin waddled into the conference room we'd reserved for the arbitration with a paper bag over their head with holes cut for eyes and beak. His ability to see could not have been ideal as he careened from doorframe to table. Eventually, with my verbal guidance—*left, right, two steps forward, and such*—my masked friend succeeded in finding his chair.

The arbitrator, a sturdy man who easily exceeded sixty years, next entered and sat at the head of the conference table, laying an overstuffed leather valise on the polished wood surface before him. He lowered his glasses and stared over them at Poirot. Poirot stared back.

"My name," the arbitrator said, "is Quinton Randolf. You will refer to me as Judge Randolf during these proceedings. By way of introduction, I've been doing this longer than most of you have been alive. In all my arbitration cases, I've learned one valuable thing. Fairness is about equality. If all goes well, in the end, everyone will be equally miserable." He shot an over-the-glasses glance at Poirot and shook his head. "Are we ready?"

Averill sat up, banged the edges of a stack of papers into alignment on the tabletop, and affirmed she was ready. The opposing solicitor slapped a file folder in front of him like the crack of a whip and also affirmed readiness.

"Gantlets sufficiently thrown," Judge Randolf said. "Shall we…" He stopped mid-sentence and pointed to Poirot. "The bag? Must we?"

Averill again shuffled her papers. "Your honor, the case we have before us is not simply one deciding property but a pivotal case in a new era for the rights of sentient beings… the tip of an enormous legal iceberg."

At the mention of an iceberg, Poirot squawked from beneath his bag.

The opposing solicitor interrupted, "Sentient? If a self-driving car drove off, would it not be returned to its…"

"Oh, please," the judge said. "Is this a masquerade party or a pantomime play? Don't answer that. Someone needs to take that paper bag off that penguin's head before I proceed."

I started to go to Poirot, but he waved me off with a little mournful squeak; then, using his flippers, he removed the bag himself. I involuntarily backed up two steps.

He was a sight. Bristles he'd glued on as a disguise fell on the floor whenever he turned his head, though most had already fallen off in patches, leaving bald spots. The markings he'd made with a permanent marker to cover the bright orange beak, distinctive to his species, were similarly worn away, leaving an irregular pattern that left the impression that he was some orange-fanged creature in need of an orthodontist. I had to admit that he cast a sinister persona.

Those on the plaintiff's side gasped at seeing him, and then their collective noggins huddled for hushed dialog. The daughter, Alto, raised her head occasionally to gape at Poirot, and I saw her make a gesture that could have been her crossing herself. Mrs. Fenn reached into her purse, withdrew a small crystal bell, and held it in front of her as one might use a crucifix to ward off a vampire. Poirot shrank into his chair as Mrs. Fenn nodded menacingly. The son-in-law, William Willowart-Nestig, leaped up from his chair and headed for the door as his spouse screamed after him, "Willie, you coward!"

Mrs. Fenn rose, gathered her things, and, pointing at Poirot, said, "I will not have that ugly, molting, disgusting thing in my house."

With that and her daughter in tow, she stormed from the room with her solicitor calling after her. Averill stood and said, "This is not acceptable. I had a case they'd write about for decades—the case to define the age. This…" she pointed at me, "is your fault!"

"Well," the judge said. "As I said, if everyone is equally miserable, my work here is done." He began to arrange his valise, then turned to Poirot. "You must be glad to be free of that rather insulting woman. But you don't seem entirely happy, either."

Poirot looked down. "I'm not molting." He put the bag back over his head.

We took our leave. Poirot waited outside while I got a to-go order from our favorite sushi place.

Within two weeks, Poirot had sufficient plumage to return him to his selfie-worthy self. But that night, we chatted through his bedroom door as we ate our

respective meals. Times I did happen to catch him out—
if he went to the kitchen or whatnot—I couldn't help my
reactions. I didn't mean to stare, but a penguin head, bald
on either side--not quite a Mohawk, is so odd that I had
to keep staring to give my feeble grey cells time to take it
in. I confess that I managed to sneak one photo, which I
take out when I need a good laugh.

# CHAPTER THREE

## POIROT AND THE CROWN JEWELS

When Poirot had first come to live with me in my rented flat, I'd left the television off and hid the remote. My concern seemed well-reasoned. He had demonstrated the occasional mania—the obsession with the Nathan's Hotdog Eating contest was but one example—so I felt an appliance proven to instill all types of desires, fads, and fashions would likely ignite grass fires in the little penguin's already unfettered id. Wildfires for yours truly to put out, rushing to the rescue, extinguisher at the ready.

Thus, it came as a surprise when returning home, groceries in hand, to find Poirot sitting on the couch with the television on.

"Ah, Hastings," he turned to speak, holding up the TV remote between his flippers. "I found it in the very back of the end table drawer. You were probably wondering where it was. It would explain why the television was never on."

Poirot demonstrated some mastery of the object by hitting pause. A rather attractive young woman in a turquoise evening dress was left frozen in an angry pose, mouth open as if yelling at the gentleman, also in evening dress, to her left. I found the image distracting for further conversation and told Poirot so. He shrugged, at least as much as one with no shoulders could manage, hit the power button, and the screen went black. Seeing that he could click it off without hesitation assured me that the damn thing had not hypnotized him. I, of course, knew he didn't quite grasp the technology and that I'd need to turn it on again to take it off pause. Besides, knowing there was an image of an angry, frozen conversation behind the blank screen would keep me from sleep.

"What did you get, Hastings?"

I realized I still held the grocery bag and brought it into the kitchen. Poirot hopped off the couch and followed me.

"Oh, the usual," I said. I took out romaine lettuce, a bag of dried lentils, onions, and such. Poirot lifted his beak, sniffing. "Yes, of course, I got the mackerel," I quickly added.

"From the fishmonger."

"Sorry, no time. I was waylaid by, well, I'll explain later, so you'll have to make do with the grocer's fare. It did look particularly fresh." Poirot had taught me how to assess fish—it's all in the eyes, and these had the unsunken bug-eyed clarity that gave one the unnerving guilty thought that if you rushed them to the nearest body of water, they'd get the old gills going and swim off.

"Fresh as fresh could be," I assured him.

Poirot shifted from foot to foot. I didn't need him to use the translator on his chest harness to tell me he was thinking, *I'll be the judge of that,* but was too polite to say it aloud.

I plated our meals: Dal makhani leftovers from last night's dinner for me and the fish for Poirot. During the meal, I couldn't help but notice my friend touching his eye periodically with a flipper and squinting. Before I could ask, he spoke.

"I think a monocle, Hastings. What do you think?"

"It would look damn dashing, Poirot, but I'm not sure you have the eye socket for the device. Not much of an eyebrow ridge if you follow me. Not to criticize," I said, pointing to and dramatically animating my left eyebrow. "The ridge needed to hold it into place is a bit of leftover primitive anatomy, no doubt from my Neanderthal ancestors." Then I held my tongue, wondering if he was asking for a monocle due to vision problems.

By my association with Poirot, I had come to know more than the average Londoner about penguins. Though my expertise might let me blaze through questions about the creatures on a TV game show, it was far from veterinary level. Concerning eyesight, I knew they, and presumably, my friend, were color blind except for blue and green hues. (*When recalling this incident, I must pat myself on the back for not launching into a dialog on the strange evolution of human color perception and the curious use of the phrase "wine-dark sea," rather than deep blue, in Homer's epic poems or the lack of distinction between green and blue in Japan.*)

For penguins, this was an adaptation to underwater hunting, and other colors were largely absent in the Arctic lands. I'd never had reason to question Poirot's visual acuity. I considered signs others might take for poor vision, such as bumping into furniture due to the inherent instability of any short-legged, top-heavy creature. But he still might suffer from myopia. After all, evolutionally speaking, would it be a survival advantage if a penguin could count the scales on the fish they'd just nabbed?

To the point of lacking closeup vision, he often spread the Sunday paper on the floor to read, walking about the pages nodding and cackling to himself. The section he was most drawn to was the obituaries, perhaps due to the images of elderly ladies and the hope of finding his original and abusive owner. Poirot had been purchased following the fashion for penguin butlers to answer the door and serve drinks at soirees. His owner tortured Poirot with a little silver bell all hours of the evening to serve her Damson Gin.

I picked up a section of the daily paper Poirot wasn't

standing on and held it close to his face, thinking I'd use it to test close vision.

Poirot immediately squawked.

"Sorry, old bean, I was wondering if you wanted the monocle in order to see close things more clearly."

"No, no," he said. "And I should also like a cigarette holder."

"But, Poirot, my friend, you do not smoke." I was about to add that it was a nasty habit when I had a thought and asked, "What television shows did you enjoy today?"

He listed a few, and I realized Poirot must have found a channel showing old American television shows. I explained that to him.

"Yes, Hastings," said Poirot. "They were all of an older time. There was apparently no color then. But it's an important record. I learned much. For example, we believe that talking animals are recent, but a talking horse preceded all this by decades. He even had a pet human named Wilber."

"Had a pet human, you say?"

"I believe he owned him, but you mustn't be offended, my friend—they were not equals as we are."

I gently questioned his assumption that there was a period in history wherein a horse might own a human.

"I agree. It is my interpretation," Poirot replied. "It wasn't explicitly drawn. Rather, one had to surmise by carefully observing the sociological clues. You see, Wilber addressed the horse as Mr. Ed, whereas the horse addressed Wilber by his first name. Further, the first name of the horse was never given, nor was the human's last name. I see no other conclusion one may reasonably arrive at other than the horse was the superior."

I decided I need not get into the logical weeds with my friend concerning an absurd television comedy and let it go. But he went on.

"And, though not a talking animal, I also saw a show where a man pretended to be a bat along with a young man pretending to be a bird."

"A robin, perhaps?"

"The very thing! I ask you this, Hastings: who imitates who in a hierarchical social dynamic? Clearly, these shows record a time when humans were not the capstone of the pyramid as they are now. Not to be critical, but their imitation of said animals merely consisted of using their names and wearing some superficial costuming. Curiously, they were the foes of a man pretending to be a penguin. Despite his equally deficient costume, that man had a sartorial style I wish to emulate."

The next day, I decided that a dose of reality would do Poirot some good, so I arranged a field trip to the London Zoo for the following week. It wasn't far from my Marylebone flat, but short walks for me were long waddles for Poirot, and the tube or bus was generally difficult, what with the steps and the unwanted attention—at least for me—so I hailed a taxi.

The entrance was at the north end, off the Outer Circle, where we endured much attention as we queued up for tickets. A smattering of potential rain clouds threatened from the west, and I must have been tapping my umbrella's handle because Poirot expressed an interest in having an umbrella for himself. I should have anticipated that because—along with the monocle and cigarette holder—it would complete the accouterments of *The Penguin* character from the *Batman* television series.

"We can shop for an umbrella for you tomorrow—and a top hat," I said, holding back a snicker as I pictured one small enough to fit his head.

Poirot raised his flippers as though feeling such an

imaginary chapeau. He held an expression of serious interest for a moment, then shook his head and dropped his arms.

"No, Hastings. I thank you for the offer, but I think not. You see, I need not fall back on mere props like a human actor to achieve this perfect penguin form." He patted his stomach and stood a bit straighter.

Poirot did not bring up the umbrella again.

In case the reader was wondering, I did have mixed feelings about his wish to emulate a criminal. Now, Poirot was a fine fellow who would do no one harm but—how to put this—the fellow's moral compass was not so much wrong-pointed as to be completely lacking. Influenced—one would reasonably surmise—by his newfound attraction to American television, he had, of late, been excited over the possibility of being in what he labeled *a caper*. On more than one occasion, I found him casing a local jewelry store. When I confronted him about it, he said I was not to worry about any planned robbery because he had deemed the goods to be insignificant plunder. He then began to inquire if we could visit the Crown Jewels at the Tower of London.

However, as to our zoo outing, we turned left upon entrance towards the Penguin Beach exhibit, which was my primary purpose for our visit. Although I had to promise Poirot that we would also see the lions before we left—he'd said something about needing muscle for whatever imaginary caper he was cooking up.

We caught the early show at the Penguin Beach exhibit. A crowd of twenty or thirty visitors stood in a sloping amphitheater before a glass wall, letting them see into the depths of a large pool. Beyond was a recreation of a rocky shoreline as one might find in the Falklands or other penguin habitats further south. Poirot scoffed at the beach motif, asking where the icebergs were. Talking animals were not so unusual these days—another guest had with her a companion bear of some small kind—a honey bear or Sun bear, but I couldn't be sure. Still, we drew attention from other visitors asking if he was part of the show. Poirot's offer to give a dramatic recitation of some of his poetry cooled all interest considerably.

Across the pool emerged four or five staff members dressed in outdoorsy, brown, park ranger-type garb. Penguins came from wherever they were—from the pool and by the rocks—and surrounded the attendants. I assume the buckets they carried had something to do with it. One, a female staff member, took to the microphone and welcomed the crowd in what struck me as an overly chipper voice, obviously aimed at the younger visitors.

We learned from the brief talk that most of the fifty penguins in the enclosure were Humbolt penguins. They were several inches shorter than my friend, a King penguin—second in size only to the Emperor penguin. Where Poirot was sleek with a distinct dark-suit appearance with a white front and clean orange markings, the Humbolts were primarily black but mottled irregularly with white splotches, and the beak truncated and a bit stubby to my eye. There were a few other, smaller species—one, the Crested penguin, was the variety that Poirot had, just months earlier, disguised himself as, by gluing broom bristles to the sides of his head in an attempt to elude capture by his previous owners.

The conclusion of the talk and climax of the show was the emptying of the buckets into the water. Silvery fishes plop, plop, plopped into the pool, followed by diving penguins, who had, by that time, all come out of the pool to surround the attendants. The people crowded to the glass to watch their antics underwater. Poirot too. Once, I saw him bang his beak on the glass when a fish swam close to him, then turn quickly, pretending it hadn't happened. I also pretended I hadn't seen this, looking off into the crowd.

When we'd tired of the penguins, we walked through an exhibit showing their various types and habitats on illuminated placards. At the end was a curious photo showing a penguin—a King penguin like Poirot—walking in parade dress in front of a line of soldiers standing at attention. The penguin's name was listed as Brigadier Sir Nils Olav III. The legend read that the photo was of Sir Nils inspecting the Norwegian King's Guard. I'd heard of this. It was a quaint custom going back decades, with the title handed down to successive penguins as they aged out, the military rank increasing with each iteration. Whatever reason for successive promotions was as inexplicable as the entire affair, so why seek to understand, except to note that if it went on long enough, the ruler of the entire galaxy may one day be a penguin. This did not escape Poirot's notice. I took the time to point out that it was only an amusing custom with little effect.

"Yes, now, but don't you see, Hastings, that history has been lying to us. This may be now reduced to what you believe to be a quaint custom, but all stories are based on a grain of truth—a remnant from a forgotten time when a penguin commanded the troops."

After this, we took a turn around the zoo, intending to wind up at the lions as I'd promised Poirot. A surprise awaited me in front of the ostrich exhibit in the form of my cousin Averill, a highly successful solicitor in London who'd, earlier that year, connived (in my opinion) to represent Poirot in a lawsuit against the company that installed the circuits that now allowed him to express his feelings in words. Her angle had been that granting speech introduced an awareness of their own mortality and thus introduced crushing existential anxiety. It had something to do with Korzybski's idea that our knowledge of the world is limited by the structure of language, and since death is an abstraction—something *to be*—animals, having no language, have been free from the fear of their own mortality. Thus, by introducing language, we, *ipso facto*, introduce existential anxiety in poor, previously ignorant creatures, such as my friend Poirot. Or not. I've never understood Korzybski and trusted that what Averill told me was a fair representation.

Other than the fear he had of being captured and put back to serve as Mrs. Gladys Fenn's butler, I've not noted any anxiety in Poirot, existential or otherwise, let alone cosmic dread.

Averill began speaking loudly, growing in intensity, and soon, she was not just talking to Poirot and me but to the group gathering around her. She pulled out a poster she had rolled up in her coat, and a young man stepped up and helped her unfurl it. It read, "GIVE US OUR VOICE!" I hadn't realized until then that those gathering were part of her cohort. It was all planned. Backing away and prodding Poirot, we made haste before zoo security showed up.

*Oh my,* I thought. Her case that posited giving animals speech caused damage—perhaps due to the lack of clients stepping up to sue to have their speech abilities removed—had gone nowhere. Now, she'd flipped to the opposite position—demanding they be given voices. Any new clientele she planned to represent in a class action could not object to her representation without first having a voice.

We beat a hasty retreat—as hastily as Poirot's little

feet could waddle, anyway.

"They won't do," Poirot said in the taxi on the way home.

"They won't do what?" I asked.

"Do, Hastings. Do for henchmen. Did you see them when they brought out the fish?"

"Isn't sycophancy a quality that any criminal genius would want in his or her henchmen or henchwomen?"

"But no," Poirot replied. "Fawning adoration to whoever holds the bucket of fish? A caper cannot hinge on such."

"I see. Any fish-bucket-wielding passerby would certainly disrupt a carefully planned caper."

"You mock me, Hastings."

I lied and said I did not, but Poirot went into one of his sulks for the rest of the ride home.

Days passed wherein I saw little of Poirot. He was in and out, and when in, I heard him in his room, talking to himself or perhaps on a cell phone, though where he'd have acquired such, I could not imagine. One day, a strange man rang the flat from the downstairs entry and asked for Poirot. Poirot asked that I let him in. When he arrived, I opened the door, asked him in, and introduced myself. I learned that the gentleman's name was Reggie. He was a tall, muscular chap with the appearance of a tradesman about him. A curious action under his greatcoat revealed that he had with him a puppy. From what I could see from its nose and face, I deemed it a dog of the Corgi variety. It emerged more fully after our introductions and squirmed to lick Reggie's face, who responded with coos and chin scritches.

"Is that Reggie?" Poirot called from his room. "If so, send him in at once."

"Scuse me, Gov," said Reggie, pushing past me and disappearing into Poirot's room.

Their meeting could not have taken all of three minutes whereupon Reggie emerged and left, thankfully taking the puppy with him. Not that I don't like puppies, but I worried that Poirot had rashly decided to acquire a pet without consulting the rest of the household— namely myself.

So, it was for the next few days. Poirot would go off without explanation, and Reggie would arrive—though sans puppies—meet briefly with Poirot and leave.

I hadn't heard further critique of the Batman television show for some time, though there was evidence of Poirot's continued television watching. I didn't want to bring it up, but my own curiosity eventually overcame me.

"I've decided, Hastings, that one who has his plans foiled, again and again, by a rather silly man and boy is not a character to emulate."

"That's sound reasoning, Poirot," happy that he'd come to his senses.

"No, I've been studying the techniques of a man who assembles a team of highly competent henchmen. They always succeed. They use disguises to impersonate and gain access to secure locations."

*Oh…* I knew which old show he meant and expressed my doubts to Poirot on his ability to construct a disguise that would make someone think he was, say, a Soviet Block dignitary.

"You've hit upon the beauty of my plan, Hastings. But you get ahead of me. We go tomorrow morning."

I indulged my friend, and we arrived early at the Tower entrance at the Lower Thames at 8:30 and proceeded to the West Gate, bypassing—at Poirot's insistence—the ticket office and the welcome center. The main gate—as anyone who could both tell time and was not a penguin would expect—was not yet open and was manned by two guards. Poirot, I had not noticed until then, had slipped on an arm band of some sort. It was blue with some scribbled insignia in black marker.

Poirot then attempted to press by the guards.

To set this scene, I should mention that the gate we were at, the Middle Tower, was not the gate to the Waterloo building entrance, which housed the vault containing the Crown Jewels. We had more entries to go through in order to get there. This gate led to the broad grassy perimeter that mostly encircled a walled complex of thirty or so towers, ramparts, and other buildings. So, two guards as security at this point were as much ticket takers as they were guards and, thankfully, were unarmed.

"Oi, what's this then?" the taller of them said when jostled by Poirot, attempting to waddle by.

"I and my human wish entry is what this is."

"It's not opening time yet, little fellow," the shorter guards said. They exchanged bemused looks at Poirot and rather threatening looks at yours truly. I held up my hands in appeasement.

"Don't you know who I am? Poirot said. "It is I, Brigadier Sir Nils Olav III, colonel-in-chief of the Norwegian King's Guard, an honored and respected military man. Dare you bar me from viewing England's Crown Jewels?"

The taller of the men clicked his radio. "Sir, do we expect a special visit from... what did you say?"

"Brigadier Sir Nils Olav III, colonel-in-chief of the Norwegian King's Guard," Poirot said, expanding his chest and pointing to his armband.

The man repeated into the radio. "A Brigadier Sir Nils Olav III, of some Norwegian unit. If I may, sir, he is a sort of penguin creature accompanied by an odd, sandy-haired gentleman."

*Odd?* I was offended, thinking of myself as quite average.

Whatever was said in return, we could not hear as the guard was listening on an earpiece. He filled us in. "He's not finding anything."

"Tell him to look me up on the internet," Poirot said.

"You heard that, sir?" Then, holding his radio to his chest, he said to us, "He's checking."

A moment later, the guard said into the radio, "That's right. A penguiny sort of bloke—one of those talking kinds. Of what breed? I'll ask."

He held the radio to his chest again and said, "He wants to know if you're a King penguin… *I wasn't supposed to say that.*" Then, loudly, "So… what kind of penguin did you say you were?"

"He's a King penguin," I offered.

"Yes, sir. His odd companion verified it." *Odd companion.* "No, sir, I can't say as I know my penguins—one from another. I'd be inclined to take him at his word. The armband you can see on his internet picture. A bit of sloppy work, but maybe that's how they do things in Norway. Yes, sir, on the right flipper. His right, I mean."

I was beginning to think that Poirot's absurd impersonation might work to at least get us in without the cost of a ticket. Car horns honked, and when I looked at the street—rather busy with traffic—a van had pulled up to the curb, holding things up. The side door opened, and a pack of small dogs ran out, whereupon the van sped off. Poirot called out, and the dogs came running, en masse, towards us or to Poirot, more specifically. There were at least six, maybe more—hard to count when in motion—and they were Corgis, not puppies but not fully grown—adolescent, I suppose one would say.

They surrounded Poirot, tales wagging.

"Oi! What's this then?" the short guard called out—it seemed to be his standard line. He tried to block the dogs' path, but they simply encircled him, panting happily. The other described the scene to whomever he was in contact with.

"Surely," Poirot said, "you recognize the dearly departed Queen's faithful companions. The Palace sent them to accompany me to view the Crown Jewels as the King and his retinue are busy with State business this morning."

"There are no dogs allowed," the guards said almost in unison—they must have had some practice.

But, whatever the rules, as for the Corgis, they were having none of it. They dashed in and out between the guards. Poirot saw his chance and went through the gate towards the inner walls. I stayed where I was. When Poirot got but four feet beyond the confused guards, the Corgis encircled him and began yipping and nipping at his toes. I realized that they were herding him but not in the direction he wished to go. Perhaps instinct took over, and my poor little friend, being the least human and, thus, the most animal-like thing in sight, became their victim. Faster and faster, they scurried around him, driving him back toward me, standing outside the gate. I backed up close to the street. In reaction, more than anything, I raised my arms, and, as if by miracle, a taxi pulled up. Fortunately, the driver was focused on me. I flung open the door to the cab, and in came an expertly herded Poirot followed by his yipping entourage. I slammed the door and then got in the front.

A healthy tip to the cabbie quelled all complaints of irregularity. I learned that any open door triggered the dogs to herd Poirot in that direction, which got us out of the cab, into the lobby of our apartments, into the elevator—a tight and noisy ride—and finally into the flat.

As long as Poirot sat motionless on the settee, the dogs lay quietly on the floor and soon fell into a sort of heavenly puppy snoring with occasional paw twitching—dreaming of their herding success, I imagine. Poirot must have been spent because he, too, fell into a deep slumber.

Although early, I poured myself a sherry and drifted off in my armchair, only to be awoken after less than an hour by someone downstairs. It was Reggie, who I'd met earlier, who'd brought one of the pups to show to Poirot. Assuming he was there to collect the dogs, I rang him in, despite my worry that he—a hefty, rough-looking character—might cause a scene and want some compensation for the use of the dogs in a caper that did not entirely turn out.

When he entered, the dogs ran to him, tails wagging and making little happy cries, and Reggie knelt down, petting them and letting them jump up and lick his face.

Poirot just sat in a sulk and said, "Hello, Reggie."

"Sorry, the caper didn't work out, Poirot. Next time, we'll get it."

I helped Reggie carry the pups back to his van. Outside, I asked Reggie—he turned out to be a well-known Corgi breeder—why in the world he got involved in Poirot's insane caper.

He laughed. "Oh, your little fellow, what an imagination—think about it a moment—what if it had worked? What's the worst? My dogs got a bit of fun. I'd parked my van and watched from across the street. You didn't see me? If that cab hadn't pulled up, I would have collected the pups."

"No, I didn't see you. There was a bit of a scramble going on."

Regie pulled out his phone. "I got the whole thing on

video. Can you imagine the views I'm going to get? Millions! I'll make a fortune, I bet. You take care of Poirot. He's a pip."

"I will, I will," I replied. "Someone has to."

"Oh, it's more than some obligation, right?" He winked, gesturing back towards his dogs with his thumb. "Keeps me young."

*I suppose so… I suppose so*, I had to admit, and went back to my flat eager to hear Poirot's deconstruction of the day's events.

# CHAPTER FOUR

ANTARCTICA

I spent much of the week avoiding my cousin Averill. When she received no replies to her messages, emails, and texts—rather than taking the hint—she rang downstairs for my flat one day. I pretended not to be home.

The problem was, I'd never been terribly good at pretending. Pretending required a stretching of the imagination. As any new yoga student can tell you, stretching something that one seldom uses is painful and exhausting work. So, I took the coward's way out and rang her in. Then I knocked on Poirot's door, announcing that Averill was on her way up. They'd met twice: once at a deposition where Averill, a barrister, planned to hijack the meeting for her own purposes, intending to use Poirot in a class action suit, and once at the zoo, where Averill and her acolytes were fomenting a public demonstration objecting to the technology that allowed Poirot, to have speech. My warning was to give my friend the option of staying in his room or coming out to greet her.

Poirot replied through the door, "When she arrives, tell her to wait, and I'll be out shortly. I have something to show her."

*Something to show her?* I took that as an ominous foreshadowing of some disastrous future collusion between the two of them.

After a moment, I opened the door for Averill. She handed me a grocery bag.

"For me?"

"God, no, Limpy. Where's your little friend?"

"Shall I announce you?" I added, applying an admittedly petty, cynical spin, knowing full well that Poirot was aware of Averill's arrival. "And," I added, "what do you want with Poirot?"

"You'll see."

"No, I won't see, Averill, not if it's some scheme of yours."

"He's a grown penguin and can decide for himself. Is this his room?"

I considered arguing that Poirot's age fell far short of the age of maturity in our legal system. But I knew that if I did that, Averill would twist me up in logic over the consideration of maturity in humans versus birds and specifically penguins and then Poirot's species, the King penguin who, it could be argued (and she would argue such,) reached adulthood when their baby fluff fell off and their adult feathers came in. With Averill, if it could be argued, it would be—cogent or not. Averill would keep going until I was worn down.

She knocked softly on his door. "Mr. Poirot, it's Averill. I have something for you." Then, to me, "Where did you put that bag?"

I was still holding it—a decidedly fishy aroma wafted from within.

"I've been to Ellis and Jones," she called out to Poirot through the door.

Ellis and Jones is one of London's preeminent fishmongers, often featured in Poirot's Mackerel odes. (*I dare not test the reader's patience, so perhaps a sample will suffice. If you've read one of Poirot's mackerel odes, or are a fan of Shelly, then perhaps this will give one the gist of it:*

> *O, for a bite of fishess! that hath been*
> *Cool'd a long age in the deep-delved ocean*)

Their location was not often convenient for me, but it was Poirot's favorite for mackerel—how Averill made that discovery, I didn't know. Though perhaps she simply selected that market due to reputation. No matter, her ploy hit the mark, the mark being Poirot, who opened his door just wide enough to waddle out as fast as his flopping little appendages could manage, closing the door behind him.

"Hello, Poirot," Averill purred. "Oh, Limpy, set the bag down, for god's sake."

I should apprise the reader of my flat's layout, should readers of previous adventures forget. A coat closet was on the immediate left when entering the flat. I had no need to take Averill's coat, for she was wearing a sort of jogging outfit even though, in my opinion, it was cool enough that day to wear a coat or at least a light jacket. The important part, though, is that we passed the door to my penguin friend's room and were now at the counter to the kitchenette on our right, where I set the paper grocery bag. To our right was the living room, populated by chairs, a couch, and a television. My rooms (including a separate office) lay beyond. Not having an architectural drawing of my old quarters, I lay this out for dramatic rather than strictly factual purposes.

"You say you brought mackerels?" Poirot asked.

"Yes, but first, a little test." She turned to me, "Fetch us a mirror," Averill said in a disagreeably commanding tone, considering she was my guest.

"Haven't got one, Avy," I replied with some satisfaction as it was true—none that I could *fetch* anyway—none that weren't fastened to a wall.

"No mirrors?" she retorted. "Are you Dracula?"

It took me a moment to work out how that related to my supposed lack of household goods.

"No," I asserted again, choosing to clarify. "I am

neither one of the unreflected undead nor do I have a mirror, at least not the portable variety that I might *fetch*. Fetch, Ave! As if I'm some breed of retriever."

"Oh, don't be so sensitive."

While we dueled, Poirot entered the kitchenette.

"I say," Poirot said, sniffing the air, his beak rising and falling along with flapping his flippers, which upthrust his body as much as three inches per bounce. "Ellis and Jones, you say? Indeed."

"Indeed," Averill said. "But we seem to be lacking a mirror."

Poirot, I had observed over time, had a distinct dislike for the absurd despite being a talking penguin—the epitome of the absurd. He stopped bouncing and sniffing. "You mock me, madam," he said. "What has a mirror to do with a mackerel?" (*This reminded me of a Lewis Carrol quote. When creating an example of an absurd question he posited: 'How is a raven like a writing desk?' Carrol didn't consider--nor could he have known at the time—that a raven is like a writing desk because Poe wrote on both. Now, how a mirror relates to mackerel remains to be seen.*)

"You have no mirror?" Averill said again to me.

"No," I said. "What I said was that I have no mirror that can be fetched."

Poirot pecked at the handle of the drawer just below the sack of fish in frustration. These atavistic penguiny traits came out under stress. Fearing an escalation, I offered a solution.

"Poirot's room has a full-length mirror on the back of the door. Shall we retire to your quarters, Poirot?"

"I... I... Mackerel, you say?" Poirot stammered.

I hadn't been in Poirot's room for weeks, and I had no idea what to expect as, lately, he'd been carefully barring the view whenever he ventured out as he was doing now, preventing our entry.

"First the mirror, and then the fish," Averill said, crossing her heart with a gesture that, in my experience, signified a prelude to a practical joke, but in this case, I felt was sincere.

 "Very well," said Poirot. "My room… Keep in mind that it's not complete. But I confess that I've wanted to show someone what I've been working on."

*What he'd been working on?* I'd heard odd noises from his room—a peculiar squeaking, sawing, and hammering. I hadn't inquired about it, feeling that it might have been an imposition on his personal space since he hadn't volunteered anything.

"Wonderful," Averill said. "Lead the way. Grab the bag, won't you, Limpy?"

I retrieved the bag she'd brought as Poirot waddled over to his door. "Don't judge too harshly. It needs a few finishing touches."

With the bag in my hand, we huddled outside his door in the hallway. Poirot reached up with a flipper (I'd replaced the round doorknobs with more flipper-friendly lever types) and flung open the door.

"May I present," he declared, "Antarctica!"

I must admit to some initial bewilderment. Within lay a rugged white landscape or, should I say, icescape. As I got over my initial shock, I found that I was looking at piles of broken white Styrofoam arranged into peaks and bergs. I vacillated between awe at what he'd done and being appalled at the sheer mass of unrecyclable trash I knew I'd have to haul to the dump when Poirot tired of his homemade arctic diorama.

"Where?" I started to ask about the sources and how he'd gotten all of it into the apartment without me seeing, but then I stopped, considering how proud he seemed of his accomplishment. Critical comments could wait.

"Um…," was all that Averill managed to utter. It was

the first time I'd seen Averill stunned into a single-syllable interjection. I enjoyed the moment. Displayed before us were insulation slabs from refrigerator-sized packaging down to rock-sized pieces—all creatively broken at the edges so as to appear natural.

"Antarctica!" Poirot said again, a bit louder, waving a flipper. Averill and I caught each other in a side-long glance, and taking our cue, we applauded, spewing accolades.

"Wonderful, just wonderful, Poirot."

"A marvel," I think I must have said.

"Would you like a tour?" Poirot said.

"Oh, yes," Averill said. "But for first, I think I might prefer to take it in as a vista. Poirot?"

"Eh?" he said with a touch of suspicion in his tone.

"I'm just thinking," she continued. "The magnitude would be even grander if we included the mirror, which gives any room—er, or continent—more dimensionality. Perhaps we should close the door to show it in the mirror. Don't you agree, Limpy?"

She would have been more likely to gain my firm assent without the nickname, so I waffled, saying, "Well… I once saw a home design television show that implied such."

"Brilliant then, let's try it." She brushed by me and shut the door. "Oh, spectacular." Then, in sotto, she asked me to hold up the bag. She reached in and withdrew the white paper wrapper containing the mackerel and something else I could not see. She opened the paper and took out one of the silvery fish. I must say, the Ellis and Jones mackerel on display was noticeably plumper than those from our local fish market—that it caused me to salivate, giving me some concern that I was becoming far too attuned with my roommate—it was a lovely fish.

Poirot, of course, was so transfixed by the dangling fish that he did not notice that Averill, in a swift, surreptitious movement with her other hand, affixed something to his chest, just above his speaking device but under his chin where he could not see it.

I immediately apprehended her scheme. It was the Theory of Mind test. Purportedly, it shows if the subject has self-consciousness or not. If Poirot, seeing himself in the mirror, fusses with the sticker—a red dot sticker in this case—it means that he sees his reflection as 'self.' Children below a certain age fail this test, which is staged by putting a dab of paint on their nose. This would be a foundational bit of information for the class action lawsuit that I knew, from earlier discussions, that she intended to bring to bear on the corporations involved in the modifications that gave animals, such as Poirot, self-expression and, therefore, the resulting existential agony that comes with self-awareness. Now, many things give me agony—cousins included—but having an advanced prefrontal cortex was not one of them. And, knowing Poirot, any self-awareness that caused self-doubt or 'agony' as he went along his merry way would be as noticeable to him as a dust mote in a field of ragweed on a windy day.

I stepped further into the room and turned, weaving my way around faux icebergs—careful not to repeat the Titanic's error. Averill, too, picked her way to the center of the room.

"Have you looked at how your masterpiece reflects in the mirror, Poirot?" she prompted.

"Oh, for hours," he said. He preened a bit in front of the mirror, then gave one of his chirpy squawks, which I knew indicated humor. "What's this?" he said, tapping his reflection where the sticker was affixed to him. "Oh, very handsome. Can I keep it?"

"It's a trick, my friend," I said.

"A trick for a treat," he replied, at which he raised up and gobbled down the mackerel that Averill had been holding by its tail.

"She was attempting a test."

"Poirot, I…" Averill started.

"No need, no need, Averill. I'm familiar with the subject—the Theory of Mind. I'll try to explain, for Hasting's sake. It's about self-consciousness. The test is often done on elephants. Seeing themselves in a mirror with an added dab of paint on their forehead makes them self-conscious—I know it would me."

"I'm not sure that's quite the point," I interjected.

"Whereas," he continued as though I hadn't said anything, "a human child under two would simply think their reflection was a playmate with a wonderous dab of red paint on their head, making them seek the nearest substance—likely baby food or their own poo—and smear on their own face in imitation. It is called a theory of mind because if the subject minds, it indicates they have a mind. It's all very straightforward, Hastings. Almost a tautology."

There we stood a moment, silently—the three of us— a barrister, a penguin, and myself in a bedroom of a London flat surrounded by broken white Styrofoam. What broke the ice, so to speak, was Averill when she took a step backward, snapping a piece of Styrofoam. Rather than being upset, Poirot began pecking at the bag holding the fish.

To my surprise, Averill said, "He's not wrong, you know."

We returned to the kitchenette, where the floor was tile rather than carpeted, and Averill fed Poirot the remaining fish. She seemed to enjoy the task, and with a bit of consternation, I could tell that Poirot delighted in her attention. I was not jealous but rather concerned about her luring Poirot into whatever plan she had in store. I expressed such, of course, after waiting for the last mackerel to descend Poirot's gullet—I've never been one to spoil someone's dinner with unpleasant topics.

"Just what is it you're up to, Averill?"

"Oh, Limpy…"

"Stop with the lame…," I started to say.

"Lame!" she said, laughing. "Was that a joke? From you? By the way, you'll recall telling me that you hate your first name and that you told me never to use it. What else shall I do? Shall I call you Hastings as does your penguin friend—*our* penguin friend, I mean?" She smiled at Poirot—smiling as much as a shark has the proper facial muscles to do so.

"I doubt he is fooled by your machinations."

"Are you?" she queried Poirot. "Are you somehow enthralled by my machinations?"

"Enthralled? No, madam," Poirot said. "But if you have some devious plan in mind that also involves those wonderful Elias and Jones mackerels, my enthrallment has found its price." With that, he gave a little bow and a wink.

"I'm an attorney…, cousin," she said to me. "I have a duty to my occupation, to the public, and to justice. Tell me, what is your occupation again?"

"Mine?" I replied. "I've told you before, but if you need me to reiterate…."

"No, no," she nodded and tapped her lips with an index finger. "It's all coming back to me. It's finance. No, don't tell me. Insurance. No, actuarial work, but more of an actuary for actuaries. Statistics are involved, but not doing statistics, and perhaps you said you have to attend many board meetings. Oh, now I recall—I fell asleep after thirty minutes."

"That was rude," I said, recalling the incident. "You falling asleep into your soup did not leave a good impression on my date for the evening."

"To be fair, she nodded off a bit too. Did you not hear her snort when she jerked her head back? You're lucky that went nowhere—she would have been a snorer."

"I don't find what I do to be the least bit boring." At that, I heard a whistling, wheezing noise, and when I looked over, it seemed that Poirot, no doubt sated with a belly full of mackerel, had fallen asleep standing up.

It came down to this: Averill, as we saw at her demonstration at the zoo, was seeking to create civic law actions against the companies involved in animal modifications. It would be huge. For reasons I failed to understand, she was dead set on getting Poirot to be her animal spokesperson. When I told her that nothing good could possibly come from it, she accused me of jealousy. She pointed out that Poirot presents well, somehow erasing from her memory the disastrous arbitration meeting wherein his previous owners fled from Poirot in terror. Being a King penguin, he was taller and more majestic than the penguins one might see at a zoo, so I saw what she meant, but he also carried with him the *imp of the perverse*. Poirot would never intentionally cause harm. I simply mean that there existed an aura of unintentional mayhem that, to his friends—and I counted myself as such—was charming but not befitting for serious legal matters.

Averill visited several times in the ensuing days, usually when I was away on business. (*A business that, if the reader will someday have the patience to allow me to explain in a few concise pages, is neither obtuse nor boring.*)

When next I heard of her project, it was that she and

Poirot were to appear on a live television news program. I had just returned from Brussels—where I found the Belgian beer more noteworthy than the sprouts or the waffles. A text from Averill sprung up on my phone as soon as I landed, informing me of their live appearance. I had just enough time to make it home and prepare a late tea with a plate of Jammie Dodgers, Custard Creams, and Jaffa Cakes before starting the television and finding the channel.

I suffered through commercials for automobiles, airlines, and Tesco. Then, the flashy graphics, which, to me, undercut the seriousness of any news programming. This show was under the banner of the host, William Spinacre. With his full white hair and Canary Islands tan, he was a venerable institution in the British news industry. After a musical intro, heavy on French horns and a ticking clock, came a basso. *Good evening, I'm William Spinacre, and this is The Report with William Spinacre.* The camera widened to reveal his guests: my cousin Averill, her brown hair swept back, appearing to be catching the wind as though standing on some Scottish cliff, wearing a smart jacket over a low-cut light blue camisole. Her modest, below-knee skirt was all that separated her from appearing as the average female Sky News presenter. Beside her, on the guest couch, sat Poirot. At least, he attempted to sit with his feet out but began to slide forward, then tilted to the right, trying to course-correct. Flippers windmilling, he wound up standing. Penguins do not have the sort of butt-in-the-chair morphology that our furniture was made for. He squatted a bit, I think, to remain close to Averill's head height as King penguins average thirty inches high, and Poirot was a typical specimen of that species.

Spinacre continued, "Our guests tonight are the barrister Averill Loughty and her pe--," he touched his earpiece, "I'm reminded that it is, in fact, her client, a Mr. Poirot. Is that correct, Ms. Loughty? Or should I direct the question to you, Mr. Poirot? I understand you have been fitted with a speech circuit."

"As have many—too many animals," Averill broke in. "Against their will. A cruel and anthropaternalistic intrusion, that I...."

I had the subtitles on the television, which supplied *anthropomorphic* when she said *anthropoternalistic*, a word I'm sure she made up for the occasion to boost multisyllabic dominance.

"I'm wondering if Mr. Poirot might tell the viewers what his feelings are on the subject. Mr. Poirot? And, may I say how handsome you look tonight? I've never seen a penguin in person, and I should say the common perception of wearing a fine tuxedo is not misplaced. You do speak, do you not?"

"He does," Averill interjected.

"I'm asking Mr. Poirot, please," the host said.

"I do when allowed," Poirot looked up at Averill. "I also write poetry."

"Poetry, Mr. Poirot? May we hear a bit?" the host asked.

"I don't think that is a good idea," Averill said. "We're here for a serious matter, not a..."

"Oh, no, no," Poirot said, tapping Averill on the shoulder. "I think an ode. Don't you, Mr. Spinacre? In the mode of Tennison, perhaps?" With that, he jumped down from the couch and began a yacking sound, which I knew to be his way of clearing his throat. I have been the victim of many of Poirot's poetic recitals, and the mention of Tennison warned of an extended assault on the audience, if not the entire English language. But the host egged him on.

Poirot raised a flipper, pointed his beak to the sky, and

began:

> *"Mackerel to the right of them,*
> *Mackerel to the left of them,*
> *Mackerel in front of them, scaley and fishy;*
> *Stormed forth with flippers and gills,*
> *Boldly they swam and well, Into the jaws of Death..,"*

"Oh, excellent, Mr. Poirot," Spinacre said, clapping politely. We should…"

"To decode for those unfamiliar with poetic meaning, I am Death in this case."

"Thank you," Spinacre said, again clapping, "but I do think we get the gist."

"Was it too strong?" Poirot inquired. "I should say that when I say I am death, in this poem, I mean it metaphorically, not meaning to disturb your sensitive viewers."

"Again, I feel the audience at home gets the gist of it, as do I. And, I'm sure no one thinks that you meant that you meant to personify mortality."

"Although," Poirot said, touching a flipper to his beak, "if vast number of mackerels should come my way, it *would* spell their doom."

"Of course…"

"There is a bit of a dance that goes with it. If I may," Poirot said, tapping the ground first with his right foot and then his left.

"Thank you, Mr. Poirot. Perhaps I should address the next question to our barrister, Ms. Loughty. Ms. Loughty, as I understand your mission, you feel that these modifications to animals—and I should say that for the sake of forthrightness that I have purchased for my granddaughter a Red panda who speaks both English and French—that these modifications are cruel."

"That is correct," Averill said, and she went on at some length. To spare the reader, I'll recap that her basic claim is that due to access to words imposed upon the animals comes the perception of linear time and, therefore, knowledge of and anxiety about their own mortality. Thus, they are burdened with dread. Seemingly to belie that point, Poirot continued his little dance during her extended screed. He seemed to have an uncanny sense of where he might move to intercept and regain the changing camera angles as they attempted to avoid him and focus on either Averill or the host. After a few minutes of this, a distracted Averill stopped mid-sentence—a trick I'd never accomplished; it made me consider taking up dance.

"Poirot!" she said. "Can we forgo your antics until I've made my point?"

"I wonder," the host said, "if Mr. Poirot is offering a counterargument via interpretive dance. He seems rather untroubled by thoughts of mortality. Is that indeed the point of these so-called antics, Mr. Poirot, and the sly allusion to a tragic battlefield massacre in your take on Tennyson's Charge of the Light Brigade, for we know how that ended for those poor souls? Replacing them with mackerels swimming rather than soldiers riding horses to their doom—genius."

"But…" Averill stammered. "He's an idiot—a literal bird brain."

"My goodness, Ms. Loughty, is this how you represent future animal clients? I dare say you should not expect a queue at your office door any time soon. Well, it appears we are out of time…."

"But…"

"Thank you, Ms. Loughty, Mr. Poirot. After this commercial break, our next segment asks the question: Why is a guaranteed living wage handout the road to despair? With billionaire financier Quinton Berkensfield."

I could see Averill stating something with much animation, but her mic had been cut.

# CHAPTER FIVE

## POIROT THE ARTIST

When I returned from a three-day trip to Antwerp, a parked panel van was at the curb in front of my building. I wondered if someone was moving in or out. To put that question to rest, what was being carried out were thin wooden crates of various sizes and shapes. I stopped one of the movers, a tall woman wearing gray coveralls— I supposed she was in her lower twenties by her neck tattoos and choice of hair color—a decidedly in-vogue appearance for someone lugging crates.

"I say," I said—using the phrase as a true indication of my general state of surprise— "from which flat are these crates coming?" I wound down in pitch and speed, with the last syllables in that sentence sounding like a film grinding down in slow motion because I somehow knew it was my flat.

"Which what?" the worker asked, setting down a flattish three-foot by five-foot crate and liberating her ear from its impeding earbud.

"No matter," I said, "carry on," noting that expression was literal in this case.

"Whatevs," she said and picked up her burden as if its contents were light as air, which, I discovered later, was, on the main true, and set it in the van.

I struggled to pull my three pieces of luggage over the curb, and the worker came over and helped. I thanked her and asked her name: Ruth, it turned out. Then I asked Ruth if, since she was going upstairs anyway if, she'd oblige me by grabbing one of my bags and save me a trip.

Ruth asked if I knew the little penguin fellow. I replied in the affirmative and added that I shared my apartment with Poirot, the very same little penguin fellow. She grabbed the largest piece of my luggage and pulled it up the three steps to the front entrance. I joined her with my remaining two bags, noting that one of my folding chairs was leaning, folded, next to the door. I would leave that mystery for now.

The elevator opened on my floor, and I saw, midway down the hall, that my door was open. Clive Busybody stood next to it, hovering like a specter awaiting his turn to possess a medium at a seance. (Not his real name but an apt sobriquet.) His name was, in fact, Brinbardy, but as one of the squeakiest wheels on the resident's committee, he deserved the mispronunciation. Short men can have a Napoleon Complex. I wonder if there is some psychological complex for the exceptionally tall that would explain Clive's behavior.

Where I tend to use my height for good—fetching top-shelf items at the supermarket for the vertically challenged—Clive had the annoying habit of looming over people. I found this especially irritating when I withdrew my mail. I'd suddenly find him looking over my shoulder, making little noises: *hmm, tisk-tisk*, or comments such as, *oh, tax office, that can't be good.* I don't know how he always managed to always be there at that moment.

And now, here was Clive, posted outside my flat.

"Hastings," he nodded to acknowledge me. "Good show, old man. Good show. Responsive. Nicely responsive."

"To?" I asked, honestly perplexed.

I'll warn the reader that this is a bit of a shaggy dog story, so I'll attempt to connect the dots with as little pain as possible. (*Although, the only dog with dots is the Dalmatian and it is hardly a shaggy dog.*)

Poirot, as earlier told, had created a styrofoam Antarctica diorama in his room. After my initial shock that he'd brought large amounts of non-recyclable white packing foam—mainly in the form of panels used to protect large-screen televisions and kitchen appliances—I had to admit I found his creation transporting. I sometimes made excuses to enter, sit, and become calmed by the faux arctic surroundings. Poirot noted my interest and assumed my appreciation might extend to my species in general. So, the day after I'd left for my Antwerp trip, Poirot had dragged a folding chair from our flat and set it up at the building entrance, to which he taped a crudely lettered sign:

*SEE ANTARCTICA!*
*Admission, one mackerel.*

This enterprise ended quickly for two reasons. First, the resident's committee for my flat's building assembled the very evening Poirot started his enterprise—more rapidly than I'd ever seen, including when storms caused a roof leak. They voted quickly and unanimously against having Poirot's, or any public attraction, in the building. And secondly, the average citizen rarely carried, on their person, a small fish, no matter how badly they might wish to see a homemade Antarctica replica.

As luck (or fate) would have it, he managed to have a paying customer before the committee ceased operations. The reason someone showed up with the requisite entry fee had its roots in recent events.

A few weeks earlier, Poirot had created a rather memorable scene on the live news interview show, *The*

*Report with William Spinacre.* Producers for the show had noted favorable audience responses. The host, William Spinacre, had also been taken by the little penguin and, at a meeting, wondered aloud if Poirot might make an interesting guest. Word went down the line, falling finally to the show's talent booker—the person tasked with finding and securing guests. That person was a titled woman named Lady Gilderd Freist-Forstcrindle. (*I'll point out to non-British readers that titles don't nessesarily equate to wealth. Most with a peerage hold jobs. I won't call them "regular" jobs—you won't find anyone referred to as 'Your Lordship' in a coal mine except as a joke. Old family connections still serve to get a foot, the leg, and the rest of the body, through the proverbial door.*)

It was rumored that Lady Gilderd was involved with the host of *The Report with William Spinacre*, William Spinacre, but I'll leave that to the gossips.

The occupation of talent booker demanded research of prospective guests, sometimes making appeals on the phone or in person. Additional leverage in the form of gifts was sometimes used to tempt reticent guests. On this particular outing, Lady Gildered had set out with a bouquet of Snapdragons (the favorite flowers of a reclusive movie star,) a bottle of Nolet's Reserve Gin for a politician, and a lunch cooler containing a half-dozen Ellis and Jones Fishmonger's mackerels for Poirot. After successfully booking the first two guests, she showed up outside my building on the day Poirot set up his Antarctic exhibit. Finding Poirot at the entrance, seeing the placard, and having the requisite mackerel, Lady Gildered asked to see his Antarctica exhibit.

Perhaps Lady Gildred had only agreed to look at Poirot's Antarctica to schmooze him into doing a second appearance on Spinacre's show. But when she saw it, she was later quoted as saying, "I was overwhelmed by its primitive and, dare I say, animalistic, outsider glory."  She had decided there and then that it simply must be shown to the world—not merely shown but meticulously disassembled and reassembled in a special showing at the Tate Modern, where both she and her husband were on the board.

I pieced this together from what Clive insisted on telling me and things I later learned. He also provided largely unwanted background gossip on Lady Gildred. Clive—spotting a minor celebrity—had apparently pestered her until she finally slammed my door in his face so she could go inside to talk to Poirot.

With knowledge of that background, I copied Lady Gildred, slammed the door in Clive's face, and entered my flat with my luggage.

I parked my luggage just past Poirot's open door, where Ruth had left my other bag, and snuck a peek into his room. My penguin friend was at the back, flapping his wings at his side—I knew it to be a sign of nervousness. I took in the rest of the room. His Styrofoam Arctic display had been almost completely disassembled, and pieces sat alongside thin wooden crates. A young man, who I assumed to be Ruth's helper due to his matching grey-green coveralls, held a black marker. He was numbering the backs of pieces and recording the location on sheets on a clipboard. I later learned his name was Billy and that he and Ruth worked for the Tate doing installations and moving and replacing art pieces. Next to where he sat was a pile of toothpicks—apparently what Poirot had used to fasten the Styrofoam pieces together—I'd wondered where they had disappeared to. Billy was not numbering the toothpicks.

When Poirot saw me, he called out my name and waddled toward me, telling Ruth and her helper to take care to number it all.

"Hastings!" he said when he'd reached me. I almost expected a hug, but that would not have been very Poirot-like. I squashed my urge to pick up the fellow and give him a squeeze. Once and only once, I did pick him up for a hug. It had not gone well for two reasons: he had reprimanded me in no uncertain terms, saying he was not a stuffed animal to be cuddled, and also because I discovered that a King penguin is far more weighty than one would expect. A visit to the chiropractor was the result. (*Let me point out that Most birds are equipped with hollow bones to allow flight, but non-flying birds are rather solid throughout. King penguins can weigh over 2 stone or more (32 pounds, or 14 kilos.) Poirot, I'm sure, exceeds the average. Concerned about his mackerel consumption, I have tried to get Poirot to stand on my digital bathroom scale. He declined, saying that he feared it would electrocute him though I suspect vanity is the actual reason.*)

"Hello, Poirot. What is going on?" Of course, I knew from Clive, but I also knew Poirot would want to be the one to tell me, and I was eager to hear it from a decidedly Poirot-centric perspective.

"Ah, Hastings, the most remarkable thing. Greatness, Hastings! Greatness has been thrust upon me. Though unknown to the world, my art reached out from my humble room and drew in Lady Gildred, an important supporter of the arts at London's most premier gallery."

"The Tate Modern," I offered. It's one of my favorite museums. I suddenly felt remiss in having never taken Poirot to visit, but I hadn't thought of him as an art aficionado.

"The very place. My installation, as she called it, will be the highlight in a special wing."

"There are Four buildings under the Tate banner, and Tate Modern itself has several rooms and exhibit halls. Did she say where?"

"Yes, yes, I'm sure she did, but must we concern ourselves about what else is there?"

What else was there is merely one of the world's most important and extensive collections of modern Western art from 1900 on. Artists include a few punters such as Picasso, Rothko, and Dali. I didn't think Poirot would mind that company, but I could imagine some squawking if his work wound up next to Dechamp's urinal. Poirot does not have the background and historical perspective needed to know why a men's urinal presented as art was important.

The Tate's Poirot's installation was to be in the Materials and Objects Hall. That hall is where the museum visitors would, according to the brochure, *discover artists from Tate's collection who have embraced new and unusual materials and methods.* That certainly fit both Poirot's choice of materials: trash Styrofoam, and his methods: attack by beak, wing, and flipper.

A representative from Lady Gildred came to the flat. It seemed they had not considered that Poirot might not have a cell phone. I agreed to be his de facto contact. There was paperwork to sign and a list of items for the artist to complete. I imagine—what with the nature of artists, ear-lopping and such—that written assurances are crucial.

"They want an artist's statement," I told Poirot after a scan of the delivered documents.

"It is to remind me of my Antarctic home," Poirot said, raising a flipper, his gaze skyward. "You may write that down, Hastings. If you wish to locate a pen and paper, I'm certain that I can repeat it verbatim."

"They expect a bit more verbiage than that it reminds you of home. (*As mentioned in earlier stories, King penguins—Poirot's variety—originate from islands north of that fabled continent and strole about on rocky ice-free islands when not diving for food. Poirot's fixation with Antarctica as his true home has long proven to be unbreakable.*)

I've been remiss in not taking you to art museums, but I hadn't thought it would interest you."

"You insult me, Hastings."

"I didn't mean to, old chum. I apologize if I made assumptions based on your television viewing tastes."

"No need, Hastings. At first, I, too, failed to see the depth evident in those humble game shows. There is much to learn from observing the human struggle to guess letters or the price of goods. I've even pondered proposing a show of my own design."

"I doubt there are enough mackerel-related questions available to fill half an hour."

"Ah, that is where you'd be wrong, Hastings," Poirot said, missing my sarcasm. "Due to the many commercials, there are fewer than twenty minutes to fill, and much of that is banter. Many are the questions concerning mackerel, their ways, their form, the unending patterns they form in schools—"

"The task at hand is the artist's statement," I said, cutting him off, "so a visit to Tate Modern is in order."

"If I must. But we must be back by seven. It's celebrity week on Countdown."

We took the River Entrance off Queen's Walks because it has lift access to all floors and a ramp for wheelchairs, prams, and, in this case, penguins. Stairs are not penguin-friendly, and my aforementioned back problems, coupled with a flightless diving bird's lack of light hollow bones, make ramps and elevators most welcome.

I wanted Poirot to see what he was getting into, as they say, with the artist's statement. One encounters a printed card near each composition that gives insight into the artist and their work. These often start with something like; *I've always been fascinated with the purity of a one-dimensional line.* Such expressions of a lifelong fascination with something or other seemed a fairly common element. I usually ignore those placards until after viewing the art. It will either resonate with me or not, and I want to first encounter the thing in blissful ignorance, as it were.

The Tate Modern is organized by movements: Surrealism, Minimalism, Post-War Abstraction, and so on. I left the Materials and Objects hall, where Poirot's *Antarctica* was planned, for last. Along the way, Poirot had few comments. He paused at Dali's Metamorphosis of Narcissus and commented, "Is this what goes on in your head, Hastings? I'm surprised humans can manage to feed themselves."

"It's a dream image." I paused and looked at him, "What do you see when dreaming? Do you dream?"

"I dream of mackerels, not giant cracked eggs, hideous retching horses, and stone fingers wearing wigs. If that is typical of what underlies the human psyche, you have my sympathies, my friend."

"Just look at the artist statements as we go along," I replied.

As we went along, following the timeline of modern art, I noted that printed statements became increasingly crucial in understanding the works. Take Damien Hirst's cow and calf in formaldehyde entitled *Mother and Child Divided*, where the explanation went on for four long paragraphs about Freud, Catholic iconography, and, of course, death. When Poirot told me he found it repulsive, I assured him that was the idea. I said that so he would not feel his reaction was naïve, which I feared might embarrass him. I could not proceed without, of course, mentioning Hirst's infamous Great White shark in formaldehyde, divided among three tanks.

"Sharks," he shuddered. "It is more than one of those monsters deserves. I should like to see it someday. An apt fate for such a horrid creature."

"Surely, you don't mean it, Poirot."

"I would rap on the glass and taunt the damnable thing with a haiku."

I feared a haiku about to erupt and tried to push us along in the gallery, but I was too late.

"A haiku, Hastings! A haiku for the shark," he exclaimed, causing visitors to turn our way. Seeing he had an audience, Poirot dipped his beak to his chest, then raised his head and, in a loud voice, intoned:

> *You look in peace but*
> *Never dead, forever more*
> *Never rotting now.*

"He means the shark," I explained to the other visitors. "Um, the one not here."

To my surprise, there was a faint smattering of applause, and Poirot bowed politely. I went on to tell Poirot more about that artist's encasements. He nodded appreciatively, saying he wished someday to see the work I mentioned with 100 fish called "Where Will It End?" When he told me that my description of that work had sparked further inspiration within him, I considered my introduction to modern art a success.

Eventually, we came to what I thought might be the stone in the shoe, so to speak, for Poirot during our journey through the realm of modernism—Duchamp's urinal. I used that very phrase to express my concern when we approached that work.

Poirot replied, "I have no shoe; therefore, I have no

stone," which I thought was rather Zen for a penguin.

"Yes, yes, Hastings!" he said excitedly as we observed the porcelain masterpiece. "Tell me. Would you say it is a sculpture, or is it what they call an installation like mine?"

"Well, you have me there. I think, historically speaking, it was considered, categorically, mind you, a sculpture. I think if he had added a few more plumbing fixtures, it would have changed things."

"…to an installation. Yes, yes, Hastings, I think I may have the grasp of the thing. Like that pile of trash over there." We had been wandering in and out of exhibit rooms and had finally entered the Materials and Objects hall. The first thing we saw, I had to admit, could reasonably be viewed as a simple pile of discarded items, but I had not read the statement.

"Trash is a bit harsh, don't you think?" I challenged.

"Doll's heads intertwined with children's stuffed animals? No, you are correct. It's more of a collection from a car boot sale than pure trash."

"I wonder how the artist curated these objects," a nearby museum patron murmured to her friend.

I found myself leaning towards what Poirot had said—that the artist must have offered a few quid for whatever remained at the end of the day of a boot sale and then spray-painted the whole mess with the same shade of orange paint used to mark trees scheduled for removal.

I left the Tate overwhelmed, as I always did after viewing great art. How Poirot was affected, I couldn't tell. My purpose was to give him a sense of what was expected in an artist's statement. So, I asked if he'd gleaned anything from them during our taxi ride home.

"I read them all, Hastings."

I had noted this and felt he'd spent more time looking at the texts that hung alongside the various artworks than on the artworks themselves.

"It's all up here, Hastings," he said, tapping his head with the tip of a flipper, "Very helpful indeed."

Poirot can type, but it's a tedious process and one that always makes me concerned for the well-being of my computer's keyboard. A flightless bird, such as my friend, has not the hollow bones of a fluttering pigeon but rather the dense-boned flippers of a swimmer, which Poirot uses to karate chop the keys into submission. So, in this case, I played secretary as he dictated, and this was the result we submitted to the Tate:

*The artist finds inspiration in an idealized heritage where Antarctica echoes in both the formal and the emotional landscape. Much is suggested beneath the surface of the piece as a sense of mystery pervades this work, challenging the viewer to attempt to separate landscape from imagination and contrast discarded Capitalist detritus with the tantalizing expectations of a declaration. Rather than vassalage to the real, we're summoned to find what feels true. By forgoing traditional artist's tools and using only beak and flipper, the technique becomes evident throughout the work, challenging traditional methods. Using only white and shadow, the monochromatic vista harkens back to Ansel Adams's, which, in his best works, transcend literal depictions. Subverting expectations, the work appears to pose questions that the viewer is invited to ponder.*

As with his poetry, Poirot had a talent for mimicry bordering on plagiarism. Still, he had the spirit of the thing and felt the statement would fulfill the Tate's requirement. I confess that not understanding his true intent, I edited it before submitting it and hoped Poirot would not read it once posted because I had removed his last lines. He'd ended his original treatise with what I felt was an unnecessary tangent about death and decay. I was sure he put it in due to our discussion concerning the shark, and it did not fit with Poirot's choice of rather sterile white foam as the medium.

A benefit and a treat for me was that I was allowed to accompany Poirot during the final setup of his work. It was a backstage pass to one of my favorite places. It was the day before his display's opening—a special Friday evening members-only event. I knew it would be ready and to Poirot's specifications because, on two occasions, both Ruth and Billy had come to the flat to go over the finer points with Poirot in his room—or at least that's what I'd thought at the time. That day, Ruth greeted us at the Tate's delivery dock and ushered us in. We went past many storage rooms where famous works sat, awaiting their turn for a bit of floor or wall space. Ruth, who turned out to be an aspiring artist herself, gave commentary along the way, though I could tell by her tone that she considered most of the stored works and those on display to lack a certain edge. It was a surprisingly long walk. Along the way, I was surprised to hear Poirot's squawks of agreement at her more dismissive comments. I wondered what she would say about his work if we were absent.

The discussion did not grow more positive when we joined Billy, who already had most of Antarctica assembled. Instead, he and Ruth complained about both the art and their jobs. Surprisingly, they had nothing negative to express concerning Poirot's work. Instead, they praised it as they finished the last bits, taking care to place toothpicks in the original holes, sometimes adding a bit of glue to affix any pieces that wanted to spin out of place.

Once finished, I felt a bit chopfallen. In Poirot's bedroom, it took up a good deal of one side of the room, but now it stood against a wall and seemed dwarfed by the size of the exhibit hall. To its right was a double access door where we had entered. Although the doors were over fifteen feet away, I felt they detracted. However, Poirot did not seem displeased, so I didn't bring up the doors.

The last piece added was the artist's statement, which Billy tacked up on the wall to the right of *Antarctica*. Thankfully, Poirot showed no interest in it. Instead, he paced back and forth before his masterpiece, pointing a flipper here and there, declaring that it looked even more grand than he recalled. Ruth and Billy also seemed happy with the result.

"So," I said to the two of them, nodding at the sculpture, "is this edgy and experimental enough for you?" Ruth's earlier comments on all but a few of the museum's works—mainly lauding only the Hirsts and a handful of others—had my hackles up.

"It…," Billy started.

"It has potential," Ruth interrupted.

The way she said potential struck me as a touch snide. I didn't care for their attitude and was grateful to see that Poirot had wandered off to observe his masterpiece from a distance and didn't hear that.

I failed to discuss remuneration. I don't know how some installation artwork, such as Christo's, gets reimbursed. How do the artists, some multimillionaires, get paid to plant umbrellas on a landscape or gateways with hanging ribbons in Central Park? With Poirot, the amount was not in the millions but large enough for me to offer to be the executor. In the end, we split the payment under consultation, with a portion for me to manage for his household expenses and the majority of the sum to go to an account under Poirot's name at Ellis and Jones Fishmonger's for both product and delivery.

On Friday night, we entered the museum's regular entrance and made our way to the Materials and Objects

Hall—a title I found a bit mundane, truth be told. The crowd was at first thin, and then, approaching the hall, the noise level increased. As we entered, people turned to see us, nudging their friends, and then all eyes watched us enter. I've always taken great care with my clothing and kept up with styles, but I'd never gotten the hang of dressing for the avant-garde crowd. Here, before us, with Lady Gildred at the center, was London's finest in dress and London's most odd—the arts community. I felt instead the staid businessman that I was.

The group, perhaps fifty or more, drinks in hand, parted like Moses' fabled Red Sea, and I let Poirot proceed to a beckoning Lady Gildred while I sought the source of said drinks. This was Poirot's moment, so I chose to watch with pride from the wings, as it were, while my friend waddled, flippers raised in triumph, toward a podium and the ramp they had kindly provided him.

Poirot had set one foot on the ramp when a young woman stepped in front of him to stand at the lectern. She leaned toward the microphone, first thanking the assembled guests and the donors—both private and corporate—and then proceeded to make an extended introduction of the director of the Tate Modern. Glancing at my watch and noting my empty glass, I returned to the cash bar they'd set up. I was third or fourth in line. Experienced with such events, I ordered another G&T without the lime wedge, usually the most reliable order in such cases, I've found. The tender, noting my generous tip from my earlier order, gave me a generous pour, which I was appreciative of later.

I made my way back in time to see the last ten minutes of the director's—I must say, somewhat rambling introduction to Poirot's work. He was a tall gentleman with a well-quaffed mane wearing neon-blue-framed eyeglasses and attired in a silver suit that, to my mind, overly reminded me of a mackerel. I had to suppress the urge to guffaw aloud at an unfortunate mental image of a giant Poirot swallowing him whole. The director, Lady Gildred's husband's brother, one Forrest Freist-Forstcrindle, Earl of Forstcrindle, had taken the microphone and stood to the side of the custom podium. It was hard to parse his talk as the room acoustics echoed annoyingly. Still, I garnered something that interested me: he referred to *Antarctica* as an installation. I would have naively classified *Antarctica* as a sculpture but accepted the director's expertise.

When he got to Poirot's introduction, it was more of a mini-lecture on outsider art and a bit on his use of recycled materials—finally, introducing Poirot as the world's first cyborg artist due to his implanted speech circuits. I'd not considered that. So, Poirot was both the first animal artist and the first cyborg to exhibit within the Tate complex of galleries. I appreciated my friend and felt the director was lauding the circumstance without acknowledging accomplishment.

Poirot was short, and the audience was tall, but I could see he was pacing nervously. (*I know that pacing implies nervousness, but I want to be clear, for one might pace with trepidation, impatience, or even anger.*)

Judging by the movements of his flippers, his mood also smacked of anticipation. It was soon to be his big moment. I knew he'd been working on a poem he was undoubtedly going over in his head. For his sake, I was hoping the intro ended soon. It did, but not for the reason I'd wished.

Suddenly, the double doors, the ones I'd felt were a distraction, banged open. In came two figures wielding handcarts bearing sizeable blue plastic drums. With surprising speed, Poirot mounted his intended podium and snatched the microphone from the stunned twenty-second Earl of Forstcrindle with his beak. Despite their paper-mâché penguin masks, I recognized the two handcart wielders as Billy and Ruth, the Tate employees who'd set up the exhibit and had been meeting with Poirot in his room. Poirot spoke:

"Art. What is art if not to cause us to face what must be faced? Disgust? Is not disgust like death?"

Billy and Ruth proceeded forward and dumped the contents of the fifty-gallon barrels onto the floor in front of Poirot's *Antarctica*. The large blue plastic barrels were filled with water, and in the water, hundreds of mackerel. They poured out in a tidal wave of slippery silver and quite dead fish washing up on the shoes, cuffs, and ankles of London's finest.

"No," Poirot yelled, "too soon. I had not read my poem!"

Billy and Ruth—heedless of Poirot's objections and the screams of patrons, some slipping and falling on the slimy fish—raised their arms in triumph, yelling, "Mackerels! Mackerels!" They began picking up fish and flinging them into the retreating crowd, laughing maniacally. I suspected that drugs were involved but, with art, as Salvador Dali once said when asked if he took drugs, said, "Drugs? I am drugs!"

I avoided being hit by a flying fish, which I would have regretted having donned one of my finest J. P. Hacket ensembles. Still, almost as tragic, one of the blighted things landed square in my half-finished G&T. Poirot was beside himself, banging his flippers on his podium and yelling as loudly as the speaker in his harness allowed. Lady Gildred's heel spike landed square on my foot. I nearly fell, causing me to spill my G&T&Mackerel cocktail down her ladyship's bosom. She retreated, fishing (*if you'll bear the pun*) down her dress. I hobbled forward, retrieving Poirot just ahead of the security guards.

As disasters involving tidal waves went, this had hardly been Fukushima. Still, Poirot descended into a funk and barely left his room for weeks. The upshot was that he was not blamed, claiming, and I have to take his word for it, that the intent was to present the barrels of fish much like Hirst's fish in formaldehyde, but Ruth and Billy took it too far and had dumped the contents. I believe his version because I could not imagine him wasting a single edible mackerel for a stunt.

The Tate was apologetic for its employees, Ruth and Billy, but Antarctica, awash with dead fish, was irretrievable. Regular deliveries from Ellis and Jones Fishmonger (*for the Tate honored their payment*) assuaged his regret, and he soon returned to the penguin I knew.

"The art world is not for me," he confided one day.

"Other fish to fry?" I asked.

"Fry fish?" he said. "Sacrilege, Hasting, sacrilege."

# CHAPTER SIX

## POIROT THE DETECTIVE

Poirot was getting…, no, had become fat. This was not simply due to the unlimited orders of mackerel from his favorite fishmonger, Ellis and Jones, that he could call up on a whim, but also due to the generous payment arrangement from selling his Antarctica installation to the Tate Modern museum. (*His work met misfortune, but the check cleared, and the Tate was reimbursed by their insurance.*) No, in this amateur dietitian's opinion, what Poirot suffered from was inertia. He had no goal, no project, and no purpose.

Since his escape from the woman who'd purchased him to serve as her butler until the time he met me, Poirot had been on his own. Granted, that was less than two days, but Poirot was the sort of fellow who strived to make his own way in the world. I admired that quality in others but would hardly wish it upon myself. Not that I've been lazing about on cushions, but swinging the old pick and shovel in the trenches of high finance was a bit more rewarding than an equal effort in a coal mine. So, having little experience in the realm of self-striving, I was at a loss as to know how to help my friend. He could seek employment, but I doubted Poirot would find meaning in most lines of work.

Poirot had never been more engaged than when he had plotted a caper to steal the Crown Jewels. Afterward, I made him promise to stay on the right side of the law. There were a few instances of backing away from the precipice of illegality. That's to be understood as, being a penguin, he was unaccustomed to human laws. As soon as I pointed out any legal issue, he would cease such activities even if it cost him time and effort. For example, he shredded boxes of lottery tickets he'd had printed and intended to sell once I showed him the salient legal statutes. (*Though I felt he'd have sold few at the price of one mackerel per ticket, with the grand prize being a thousand mackerels.*) After that, he ran his ideas by me before taking action. His schemes tended to have unsurmountable issues, such as putting on a musical entitled *Penguins* that was a transparently plagiarized version of Cats (*The lyric, "Mackerels all alone in the moonlight," was a bit beyond even for Poirot*) or using trained badgers to dig for diamonds in a nearby park. (*I was able to stop him before too much vegetation was uprooted.*) To his credit, once things such as copyright laws and basic geology were explained, he took disappointment well—this, I think, because of his confidence that another great idea would be forthcoming.

During this time, he began watching less television— declaring it puerile, except for his favorite game shows, which he claimed enriched his understanding of human nature—and took to reading. Up to then, his literary tastes had been the romantic poets (*mainly, I felt as grist for his odes about mackerel.*) I had set up a little bookstand to hold a book. I had a fine and varied selection of topics, but he was drawn to mystery novels. He'd started with Poe and, of late, was particularly drawn to what they call *cozies.* Agatha Christie was a favorite, but he declared his namesake too full of himself (*'fussy' was a damning word he used one day.*) Our Poirot was more of a Miss Marple fan.

It was a winter of, if not discontent, then at least ennui.

Fate often showed itself in the most unlikely ways. One evening, there was a repeated knocking on the door. My sudden, aggravated door opening caught the offender poised for another knuckle rap. It was a neighbor from the floor above, Clive Brinbardy, aka Clive Busybody. Upon seeing me, he gasped an inhalation as if he'd swallowed a fly.

"What is it, Clive?" I asked. "Could you not have called first?"

"I…," he managed to get out before clearing his throat. I waited patiently, wondering if he had indeed swallowed a fly. "For one," Clive managed, "I haven't got your blighted number. It seems that the one you put on file for the building directory rings some *office*," saying the word *office* as though it were contemptible. "And two," he continued, "I can't find my bloody phone. You haven't seen a stray phone about, have you?"

He said all that while peeking over and around me as if expecting to enter my flat. Clive was an exceptionally tall fellow, and it made me feel like I was the target of an amorous giraffe.

"I guarantee—your phone—is not here," I said, dodging left and right. "Further, I haven't seen an unaccompanied cell phone anywhere. And wait a minute," I said, recalling his complaint about reaching my office and not me, "why knock on my door looking for your phone? You've never been in my flat that I can recall. And when did you try to call me earlier, and why?"

Just then, Poirot waddled up beside me.

"The first is easy," Clive said. "You're the only tenant likely to be home at this time. And, no, of course, I don't think my phone is in your flat. I wondered if you'd seen it about and, if not, if you'd be kind enough to try and ring my cell phone."

That sounded reasonable, but I still wondered why he had tried to reach me earlier, so I asked him.

"Why did I call before?" Clive replied. "Oh, some association business, I'm sure—how you were going to vote on fees, elevator repair, or whatnot. But why not?"

*I could think of several reasons.*

"It was some time ago. But this… this missing phone is most upsetting. I was expecting a call from a friend of my Aunt's. I've searched my flat from top to bottom," Clive said, wringing his hands, which were at my eye level due to his height. The sight of his squirming fingers turning white as the blood was squeezed from them spawned images of some horrid sea creature one might observe from the window of a bathyscaphe. I felt a bit nauseous.

"Ah," said Poirot, looking up at Clive, "searching with sight is not the same as searching with sound." He pantomimed the appropriate senses by touching a flipper to his eye and then his ear—or I assumed it was his ear. Penguins do not have the prominent shell-like exterior auditory structures as we have, so I had to take his gesture as confirmation of its location.

Clive looked a bit lost.

"I mean," Poirot said. "Why not simply call it and locate your phone auditorily by its ring?"

Clive started to respond when Poirot interrupted, holding up a flipper. "My question was rhetorical. Obviously, you require a phone to call your phone. We will solve this by having Hastings call your phone, won't we, Hastings? It's all very elemental."

I did not want to do what Poirot suggested because that would register my number on Clive's phone. The idea that he could call me directly in the future was unpleasant. The number I'd given the housing committee for the building's directory had been my office number, which my secretarial staff would filter.

"I don't know what I can do for you, Clive," I said, putting a hand on the door.

"Why," Clive said, "precisely what your brilliant penguin friend suggested. Call my phone so I may locate it acoustically."

I reluctantly retrieved my phone from my inside jacket pocket and asked for Clive's number.

I typed the digits and put the phone on speaker so we could all hear.

"But no, Hastings," Poirot said. "Turn off the speaker. The idea is that we hear the phone of Mr. Brinbardy, not your phone."

I hung up, saying, "Why? It's ridiculous that his phone would be within earshot of this apartment."

"Indeed, Hastings," Poirot said, "which is why we must go to the apartment of the phone's owner while you redial. You may come along or stay here, but you must continue letting the call ring and redial if an answering message arises. Let us, therefore, conduct a sonic search of his flat at once. Are you coming, Hastings?"

I went along. The chance of seeing the interior of Mr. Busybody's abode seemed to me a revenge of sorts for all of his nosiness.

His flat was on the fourth floor, one above mine but not directly above. When we exited the elevator, Clive held one key from his key ring, pointing forward at arm's length as he walked, as if it were leading the way, like some divining rod. When we reached his apartment, he stopped, took a deep breath, unlocked it, and pushed open the door.

Clive ushered Poirot and me inside and then closed the door. His apartment had a similar layout as mine, as we were first in an entry hall. This led to the main room with a couch, coffee table, and sitting chairs, all a bit more ornate and multicolored than I preferred, and certainly not what I expected because Clive dressed in a way that I can only describe as indistinct. Glancing out the window, I noted that my view of the park was far superior. At the far end of a couch stood a birdcage on a stand—

unoccupied. Bookcases took up one wall of the room, and in spaces between bookends stood statues. By their excess appendages, I took them to be Hindu deities—more of the same adorned the fireplace mantle. Considering my general impression of Clive, I had questions. And, what would have remained unspoken for me was spoken by Poirot. He had been perusing the bookshelves, at least as far as his four-foot height would allow.

"Ah," Poirot said. "An interest in mysticism of the Far East. In particular, of the theosophical bent, judging by this book by one Madam Blavatsky." He pointed a flipper at a doorstop of a tome on the second shelf from the bottom.

"Oh, gads, no," said Clive. "Not me. Far from it. I find it all rather goosebump-inducing. You see… oh, blast…, this is somewhat of an embarrassment…"

An embarrassment? I could hardly wait.

"You see," he said, "I'm sitting the flat for an aunt, my mother's sister. It's been more than two years living with this," he gave a wave, incorporating the entire room. "I'm forbidden to change a thing."

Poirot pointed a flipper to the bird cage.

"It was an African grey," Clive responded. "It's with her on her travels. When she returns, I can be free from this dreadful obligation and truly have my own place."

"So, she is missing? I refer to your Aunt, not the parrot." Poirot said.

"Is my aunt missing?" Clive stroked his chin. "It was over a month since I last heard from her. And that was a letter."

"And is that not a more important issue than this missing phone?"

"Yes, but… you'll both laugh." Clive looked at each of us in turn and gave a little nervous laugh. We did not laugh, but I'm ashamed to say I hoped this presaged something laugh-worthy.

"My aunt is somewhat of a mystic," Clive said. "I think I'd know if something happened to her. I'm no psychic, but I can feel her. Some days more than others. When it's 'more,' I try to be elsewhere. Sometimes, I can feel some presence as I come down the hall."

Ah, that explained Clive's odd behavior when approaching his door. All well and good, but I became concerned that we had lost track of the purpose of being in Clive's apartment. It was called 'Mission Creep' in management circles. I took out my phone and said, "Look here." Then, having their attention, I pressed *Send.* I held it to my ear briefly to verify Clive's phone was ringing, then held it to my body so we might hear the other phone. We did not.

"It is ringing, I assume, Hastings," Poirot said. "Clive, go to your bedroom and see if you hear anything. It would be muffled if in or under clothing, a pillow, or bedding."

Clive returned from his bedroom and shrugged. Then he went from room to room and opened each of his three closets. As Clive completed that, Poirot drifted back to Clive's bookshelves as much as one may drift in a waddle. I should say they were not Clive's but rather those of the missing Aunt.

"I didn't hear my phone," Clive reported.

"I'm sorry," I said. I was about to make our excuses and leave when Poirot piped up.

"Tell me, Mr. Brinbardy," Poirot said, "how long has that window by the birdcage been unlocked?"

"Is it you say? I never noticed."

I glanced over and could see, even from where I stood, that the latch for that window—a simple bevel sash lock—looked to be turned to the open position. I could not fathom why that mattered to Poirot and why it was worth a mention. We were on the fourth—Americans would say the fifth—floor, and there was no balcony, as the fire escape was through the bedroom window in all of the flats in the building. I was a bit miffed that Poirot's curiosity delayed our leaving.

Poirot pointed to the couch and asked, "May I?" to Clive. Without waiting for a response, Poirot leaped onto the sofa, reminding me of penguins in nature films, leaping up from the ocean onto rocky seaside cliffs—one of the few times I'd observed raw penguin-like action from the little fellow. Now eye-level with the sash lock, he inspected the area from side to side, occasionally poking with his beak, grunting affirmatively. Suddenly, using the couch as a trampoline, he did a little spring and then a hop and spin to turn in place, facing us.

"It is as I feared," he pronounced when he landed his pirouette, "Monkeys!"

"Monkeys?" I couldn't keep the scoffing tone out of my voice.

"Yes, monkeys," Poirot repeated his accusation, this time with a flipper raised for emphasis.

"Oh, my good fellow, must you?" I let out a little inadvertent laugh because, at that moment, I thought of the pun of *Poirot* and *pirouette*.

"This is no matter for amusement, Hastings," Poirot said, turning and letting himself down from the couch.

"I am sorry, Poirot. Could your conjecture have anything to do with the incident in the park with the monkeys?" The week before, we'd gone to the park for a stroll. We came upon a group of school children, each with a pet Capuchin monkey dressed in matching school uniforms and fitted with speaking devices. Poirot had been quickly surrounded by eight children and an equal number of monkeys (though it's difficult to estimate the exact number of either children or monkeys mid-frolic.) The monkeys displayed handstands and other simian feats of acrobatics. Fitted with voice modules, they made little jokes about Poirot's ungainly waddling gate.

"No," Poirot insisted, "it is a logical assertion. Who else could climb up the side of a building?"

"If not due to your dislike of those rude monkeys, may I put forth a suspicious influence from your recent attraction to detective stories? Was it not in Poe's Rue Morgue story where the culprit was a monkey?"

"Ah, but that was not a monkey, Hastings; rather, it was an orangutang. You would know the difference if you saw one. They are quite orange. Hence the name."

I decided not to comment further on the topic or the venue. We had done as requested, and unless Clive's phone was turned off, silenced, or the battery dead, the phone was not in the apartment. I made my apologies to Clive and attempted to leave.

"Wouldn't you like a spot of tea for your troubles?" Clive asked. He seemed nervous. I declined, and Poirot and I left, although I had difficulty dragging him away from the bookcase.

When we got back to my flat, Poirot retired to his room, and I attempted to put Clive's missing phone problem out of my mind and was somewhat guilty that I felt happy for the outcome because if Clive's phone continued to remain missing, he would not have my cell number.

It was just after five, so I fetched a bottle of Fuller's London Porter from the wine cooler and poured it into a tulip glass. I admired the creamy two-inch head of foam a moment before picking up a serviette from a drawer and fetching the leftover half of a cheese toasty from Morty & Bob's from the under-counter fridge. The list of foods as good cold as leftovers is short: pizza, enchiladas, and a good cheese toasty. I took my odd bounty to the living room, set the beer on a coaster on the cocktail table, picked up the remote, and turned on the television to BBC One, hoping for the wrap of the day's financials. I was about to take a bite from my sandwich when the word *burglary* caught my attention. The news team went on about a rash of burglaries showing red Xs dotting Chelsea." (*Please excuse the mixed metaphor, as a dot is not an X and no one says 'dot marks the spot.'*)

"You see!" Poirot startled me. He'd padded up behind me without me noticing and now peered at the TV, his beak barely over the back of the couch.

The TV went to the inevitable commercial, which I promptly muted.

"I say, Poirot, can't a fellow enjoy a snack and a bit of television?"

Poirot came around the end of the couch and stood by the coffee table.

"We must go back to the park tomorrow."

"To see the monkeys, I assume. You can hardly suspect them; they're trusted with the schoolchildren."

"You are probably correct," he said, and I caught a hint of disappointment. "However, they may know something. I think they will be of use in our investigations. We must be prepared. We must bring bananas. For bribery," he added after noting my dumbfounded look.

I expressed my disappointment that Poirot would fall for the notion that, because they were monkeys, they would fall under our spell at the mere sight of bananas.

It isn't that I'm particularly uncomfortable with being proven wrong. Still, as I sat on a park bench doling out bananas, swarmed by a virtual herd of wiry Capuchin simians, I had to admit it. The calls from their owners, a group of eight-year-old schoolchildren, went unheeded. The monkeys were focused only on Poirot, standing on the park bench, directing me in the distribution of said bananas. While I was under the command of an aquatic bird, relegated to playing exchequer to a pack of monkeys, I couldn't help thinking that something was terribly wrong with the universe.

Poirot, to his credit, had not lost track of his mission. He asked each monkey, in turn, if they'd heard anything about the robberies before giving me the okay to grant a boon. When we ran out of our tropical yellow incentives, Poirot and I exited.

"Well?" I asked when we'd gotten back to my flat.

"They knew nothing of Clive's phone nor the robberies in Chelsea," he said, but his tone made me sense there was something else. "I have made an important connection to a network of informants. They will contact me if they hear anything. We must be prepared."

"Prepared?" I inquired.

"Indeed, Hasting, prepared. We must visit a grocer and procure a large stock of bananas."

Sitting on the couch the following evening, I heard a faint tapping at the window and put the television on mute. There it was again.

"Don't just sit there, Hastings. Open the window." It was Poirot. He'd been in his room, but his keen hearing had alerted him.

I went to the window and was startled to find a monkey clinging to the brick sill—presumably one of the monkeys from the park. When I unlocked the window and slid it open from the bottom, the strange creature swung his legs in and sat within the open window frame. Apparently, Poirot had been right, and scaling the brick edifice had been nothing to a small monkey.

"Ah," said Poirot, "Agent Four, what is your report?"

"I may have something," the monkey said in its high, reedy voice while reaching out a hand as if supplicating alms.

Realizing that was my cue, I retrieved a banana from the pantry.

When I returned, I saw more creatures clinging outside and framing my window. I performed an unofficial census, went to the pantry, and returned with four more bananas. I distributed them equitably, and they left. I went to the window and saw the little simians clambering down the rough bricks as easily as if it were flat ground.

"Well?" I prompted. "What did he say?"

"They have located the thieves and their headquarters," Poirot said.

*I wondered how many bananas it would cost us.*

According to his informants, the Chelsea burglars were not the monkeys he'd suspected, but instead, they were ordinary humans with extraordinary burglary skills. They resided in a houseboat currently tied up at the west end of Cadogan Pier—the east end of which served as the Putney to Blackfriars RB6 Uber Boat transport dock, and it was common for various boats and barges to be tied up at the landing. This pier was conveniently south of and adjacent to the Chelsea neighborhood, where the news reported the rash of robberies via Oakley Street.

"I'm not sure what we can do, old friend. I think it's time to call in the authorities." However, I wondered how seriously Scotland Yard would take a report of a pack of monkeys as told to a penguin. "We'd have to catch them in the act somehow, and I think that's a bit out of our wheelhouse."

"Ah," Poirot said. "But must we? The answer is

obvious. Think, Hastings!"

I thought I was thinking, so I was somewhat insulted and told as much to Poirot.

"You have my apologies. You are not as immersed in the study of the criminal mind as I am, so I agree that it is not obvious."

What he claimed as *study* was simply him entertaining himself, reading from my library of mystery novels. They were hardly scientific theses on real-world criminal behaviors. But I could see how our dialog and this investigation were animating my friend. I suspected that his monkey informants were merely stringing us along. But, for the price of a bit of my pride and a bunch of bananas, I deemed it worth seeing Poirot revived from the low state he'd been in.

In the world of the novel, I was now in the position of the dimwitted associate who only existed to allow the detective to spout exposition without annoying the reader. I decided to let myself fall into that role to play along.

"Please obviate my ignorance then," I said.

"Obviate?" Poirot said, puzzled for a moment. "Ah, a clever pun, Hastings. To hatch the proverbial egg!"

I squinted painfully but let it go.

"The questions are these," he continued. "Why a boat? Why remain in the area? We know that burglaries have been occurring for several days. Would not the thieves be concerned with being caught with their booty?"

"They could escape on the boat if caught," I said. I felt duty-bound in my role as the dim-witted sidekick to provide an easily deflatable idea.

"Come, come, Hastings," he peered at me suspiciously. "Police patrol boats could easily catch up to any craft designed to have people living on them. No, it is to have the means to scuttle said booty if caught, sending their ill-gotten gains to the bottom of the Thames."

His idea that the criminals chose a boat as their point of operation, so they had a quick means to jettison evidence, surprised me. I could not recall a story, whether in writing or television, where Poirot may have heard of it. The water depth in the Thames at high tide could be over twenty meters or sixty-five feet. (*Britain is a hodgepodge of metric and imperial—pints, liters, pounds, kilograms, or stones depending on what was measured.*)

Losing ill-gotten gains would be preferable to jail.

I found myself impressed. I sensed some merit to his logic. Perhaps detective deduction was his hidden talent. I looked at my friend, and he was practically levitating.

I asked Poirot not to take any action until I consulted with my solicitor cousin Averill and an old friend, Robert, who was an inspector at the Yard. I had some idea of how things work, and I doubted the police would do anything based on the say-so of a gang of monkeys.

I called Robert first and caught him at home.

We caught up on incidentals, and then I broached the subject with him. To my surprise, he was fully aware of this gang and the boat they used as headquarters. They were having a problem getting enough evidence to obtain a search warrant. Partially because the owner of the boat was suing the crown for previous warrants, which showed no material results—he suspected they kept their booty suspended in some bag or container that could be quickly scuttled at a moment's notice. The whole business was an irritation for the thieves.

After completing my call, I wondered if trespassing laws would apply if Poirot went aboard a boat uninvited. After all, if a seagull landed on the deck of their boat, it couldn't be accused of trespass. I explained my thoughts to Poirot.

"You compare me to a seagull?"

"Only in the eye of the law, my friend," I said hastily, knowing how he felt about seagulls. Some months before, an incident of a mackerel snatched in a dive bomb had set him against their entire genera.

The next day, Poirot and I called on Averill at her office. She seemed happy to see Poirot, though Poirot was still not pleased with her because of her earlier attempts to draw him in as the proverbial poster boy for her talking animal rights campaign. He huffed and put on a show of disliking her attentions until she—knowing of our visit ahead of time—produced a fine selection of his favorite sashimi. Then he warmed considerably. When I asked about Poirot's legal status as a trespasser, Averill demonstrated why she was as successful as she was. She cited, from memory, examples from Common Law going back to William the Conqueror and later Henry II concerning the culpability of an animal or its owner. (*Apparently, 'ius commune' is the more accurate term as opposed to 'common law' as judicial precedent, but Averill got into the legal and historic weeds, and I wish to simplify for the reader.*) It was all a bit troubling. In Medieval law, they could accuse the instrument of a crime of the crime. She cited an example of putting an axe in jail for murder. I asked if that odd logic could apply to Poirot.

"The important distinction here," she said, leaning back in her chair, fingers steepled, "is that Poirot is in a grey area, being neither a trained pet, say, a crow trained to steal jewelry, nor a wild animal who might do damage, trespass, or cause some other harm due to its ignorant nature."

"So?" I prompted.

"As you say, the police can't seem to get enough

evidence for a search warrant. If some *"wild creature…"* (she used air quotes—I'd warned her ahead of time about using a Seagull for an example) "…went on the burglar's boat, it is not trespassing. Any evidence exposed to public display due to such action could be used. For example, if a wild bear or badger dug or tore into a shed, revealing a hidden cache of stolen goods."

Poirot looked up from his feast, "I doubt we'll find a bear on the docks of Chelsea, and badgers dislike water."

"It's an example," Averill said.

"A more realistic example would be a dolphin," Poirot said. "They are far from the gentle creatures, people think. That maniacal laugh. Is it not enough to chill even the bravest heart?"

"But, what of Poirot," I asked Averill in an attempt to get back on track. "Would any evidence he found be admissible in a trial? And, more importantly, could Poirot be charged with a crime?"

Her next words did not fill me with confidence.

"Let me just say that I can't wait to represent Mr. Poirot in this groundbreaking case."

Despite the lack of legal clarity, there was no way to dissuade Poirot, and the following Friday evening, I found myself with Poirot at Cadogan Pier. We met Robert, my friend from the Yard there. Two officers accompanied him to ensure our safety.
Robert had told us that the typical times of the recent rash of burglaries were in the evening on Friday or Saturday nights when householders would likely be out to dinner, visiting friends, or at a show. (*The Yard later learned that there was some connection to the burglaries and inside knowledge of ticket purchases for shows at the West End, guaranteeing some hours where the occupants would be absent.*)

Therefore, we felt we had a good chance that the

burglars were not on their boat.

Poirot didn't warm to the inspector, being convinced that his own network of monkey spies had made the discovery. He explained that the inspector had extracted the idea from conversations with me. I had tried to tell Poirot that Robert knew about the burglar's houseboat lair when I'd called him, but Poirot said that Scotland Yard inspectors are very clever and had somehow tricked me into thinking he had known all along. Needless to say, Poirot had a strong sense of ownership of the project.

It was a fine evening with only a scant mist dampening my raincoat. Poirot, of course, was grumbling. We stood dockside of a thirty-foot boat that I'd call a barge but for having a wheelhouse and cabins above the deck line. It was painted with a broad stripe of red at the gunnels with a powder blue trim around doors and windows; the rest was dark wood with a dismal, waterlogged appearance. Faint interior light barely illuminated the windows a dull orange. The landing end of the gangplank squealed whenever the boat moved slightly. A simple garden gate bearing a no trespassing sign barred passage.

Poirot waddled over to the gangplank without preamble and lifted the simple latch on the gate. Immediately, our little party was painted with light. I should have realized—no, my friend, Robert, the inspector, should have tweaked—that any burglars adept at bypassing the often-advanced security alarms of their wealthy Chelsea victims would not leave their abode and its presumed ill-gotten gains unguarded.

A quavering voice called out, "Who goes there?" as what appeared to be a llama (*I discovered later that it was an Alpaca*) raised up and looked down from the boat above.

Undaunted, Poirot swung open the gate he'd unlatched and made good time going up the gangplank in energetic hops. The boat's guardian, upon seeing this, raced to the stern of the boat, effortlessly passing by before Poirot reached the top. We heard a loud splash.

"Poirot!" I called out. "It's no use. They've scuttled their booty." He nodded and made his slow, ungainly walk down the gangplank.

The creature reappeared and made humming kazoo sounds, which I took to be laughter. This made Poirot's ungainly walk back down even more pathetic, and I imagined that if he had shoulders, they would be in a full slump.

"Perhaps we can get a scuba team out tomorrow," Robert said. "Lot of good that will do."

I asked how deep the water was and if the current was strong.

"Not a strong current and maybe twenty feet if the tide is high. Why?"

I pointed to Poirot, who had rejoined us.

"In the wild, my friend's species have been known to dive up to eighteen hundred feet," I said this, knowing that the deepest water Poirot had experienced was his bathtub in his room's attached bathroom.

"What say you, Poirot?" the inspector asked.

Poirot puffed out his chest. He turned to me. "I will be brave, but we must prepare a bath for me when we return, Hastings. God knows what filth is in this water." With that, he dove.


With the retrieved bag, Robert and the Yard were able to make enough of a case to get a search warrant and find evidence to charge the gang of burglars.

Averill called me at first light the next day. She was livid. She'd just seen the news report of our adventures the night before.

"It could have been a landmark case!" she whined.

"He did trespass a bit," I mentioned that he'd gone to the top of their gangplank.

"But, no one pressed charges," she said and hung up.

Poirot, for his part, got his bath upon return to our flat. He was effusive in his description of his dive.

"I tell you, Hastings, it was like flying. Wondrous."

I refrained from pointing out that because he was a flightless bird, it was a rather poor simile. Just then, my phone rang. I absentmindedly answered before checking who it was. It was Clive.

"Sorry to bother you at such a late hour, old bean," he said. "I wanted to tell you that I found my blasted phone. I knew it might prey on your mind. Would you like to know—it's so silly—where the damnable thing was?"

Though I didn't care where the *damnable thing* was, I considered the expediency of simply saying *yes*, which I did.

"It was in the blasted laundry I'd sent out. Can you imagine?"

I confessed that my imagination was sufficiently deficient on that point, told him I was happy he had found his phone, and wished him well.

"It's all for the good, you know. It was traumatic, but one good outcome is that now I have your cell phone number. Karma, as my auntie would say."

"Yes, karma," I said, looking over at a well-satisfied penguin and hung up.

# CHAPTER SEVEN

## POIROT AND THE CRYPTOZOOLOGISTS

Poirot's business ventures rarely went beyond the printing of business cards. The latest being *Poirot, Private Investigator*, an occupation for which he had notable success—getting the goods on a gang of burglars with the help of Scotland Yard and a pack of monkeys. Yet, despite the notoriety, the phone did not ring. That Poirot had no phone might have had something to do with it. Poirot had not followed up by applying for a P.I. license, registering as a business, or getting a phone. All effort was applied to the design and printing of two boxes of business cards. Meetings with a graphics designer and the printer, who, thankfully, was within walking distance, even for a penguin, went on for weeks. Ultimately, it simply read "Poirot Investigations" in a raised fourteen-point Fairwater script (*Chosen over the Edwardian ITC font for being more readable.*)

When I remarked on the lack of contact information, he explained that any prospective client who did not know everything there was to know about the famous penguin who broke the Chelsea burglary case was not worthy of his time. These cards soon joined the boxes of other business cards: Poirot, Installation Artist; Poirot, Impresario; Poirot, Poetry Recitals; Poirot, Television Personality.

That last one, *Television Personality*, was from his appearance on the news and interview show *The Report with William Spinacre*. He appeared for the first time with my cousin Averill as a prop for her proposed class action suit on behalf of talking animals, but the host took more interest in Poirot and his odes than in Averill and her cause. Recently, Spinacre had him back to discuss the Chelsea burglary case, which should have been a memorable segment wherein Poirot could have spun a remarkable tale of daring-do but for his insistence on sharing the spotlight with his gang of undercover Capuchin monkeys who, in the confusing environment of the television studio, behaved as well as expected, which, to put it bluntly, was not well at all. (*Until then, I'd assumed that their habit of throwing their excrement was some anti-ape propaganda.*)

Lately, my friend, lacking a card-worthy occupation, busied himself reading, watching television game shows (which he labeled as research into the human condition,) and, most surprisingly, visiting with our upstairs neighbor, Clive. However, it seemed not so much to visit with Clive as to avail himself of his Clive's aunt's collection of occult Theosophical Society books. Poirot seemed less interested in their typical claptrap of auras, rays of creation, and mystical powers than in their view of human history. Their founder, one Madam Helena Blavatsky, was notoriously opposed to Darwinism, keeping a stuffed baboon in her apartment, which she'd named Darwin. I suspected that what appealed to Poirot was her fabrications of alternate explanations for human history. This, I was sure, was what Poirot was after. More than once, he'd proposed that penguins had once ruled the earth. I took such assertions in stride. I would hold off any counterarguments and simply reply that while no one could prove such an assertion wrong, Poirot had no evidence that it was true. He countered that evidence was unavailable because Antarctica (his proposed penguin Eden/Headquarters.) was now under hundreds of feet of ice.

Rather than leave it at that, which would have been wise, I pointed out the difficulties of smaller beings bossing larger ones around. His rejoinder was the recent news of fossil discoveries of now-extinct seven-foot-plus penguins. These creatures were aptly named Colossus penguins (as the names King and Emperor were already taken.) I pointed out that humans had hands and could wield weapons, and Poirot replied that Colossus penguins were themselves weapons. At that point, I was kicking myself for participating in one of his absurd arguments. Wishing to extradite myself, I finished by saying that we'd just have to wait for the Antarctic ice sheet to melt to see who was right. (*That should give me decades, depending on the rate of global warming, to produce counter arguments.*)

But that wasn't the end of it.

"Because the continent is largely unexplored," Poirot said. "It holds many mysteries. Can we say that the Colossus species is extinct?"

"Oh, please, Poirot. None have been seen in all of human history."

"Ah, but is that not also what is said of the elusive creature, Bigfoot?"

"They don't exist. Likely confused for bears. I mean the other way around."

"Confused for…" Poirot scratched his beak with a flipper and nodded. "Ah, Hastings! You have stumbled upon it!"

"No," I said, vainly attempting to ward off what I feared he might say next.

"Yes, Hastings! Yes! Who can say that the animals thought to be Bigfoot are not, in fact, giant penguins adapted to a northern woodland environment?"

Days passed, and Poirot handed me a flyer. It announced that an international cryptozoological conference was being held at the Hilton ballroom the following evening. I agreed to go for two reasons: concern over whatever trouble Poirot might stir up (I've found that a strong belief plus an inability to prove that belief is a volatile combination.) And also for my personal amusement. I didn't mean I intended to laugh at people who believed in the Loch Ness Monster and such, but that such outre beliefs are inherently amusing, even when taken as wonderous fiction. I also expected many colorful characters to attend, though none more colorful than Poirot.

We took a taxi to the Bankside Hilton and entered through the lobby. The people queued at the hotel's central check-in seemed of a disappointingly regular sort. Then, I saw a placard that directed us to our event's location, a hallway leading to the many ballrooms. I wondered when this or any hotel ballroom had last hosted a ball. They were now mainly used as meeting and lecture rooms—for those touting self-help, product announcements, or anything that needn't require a full-blown convention hall. This cryptozoological convention used four rooms for breakout sessions. One had to choose one of the four lectures for each period, and there were two sessions. Two of the first sessions were on Bigfoot, and Poirot and I struggled over which one to attend. One of the talks was on Bigfoot and UFOs; the other was on the Yowie—the legendary Bigfoot of Australia. We opted for the Yowies. One of the second session lectures was on Bigfoot sightings in Great Britain, and also decided on that one. I wondered if Poirot would claim that Robin Hood was a Bigfoot. (*When I jokingly posited that, he said Robin Hood's large rotund associate Friar Tuck was the more likely suspect.*)

We left the lobby, went to a hallway leading to the conference rooms, and stood in line to register at a table.

Poirot was not the only animal. An ostrich was queued up in front of us. Nervously, it turned this way and that, and its tail feathers brushed over the top of poor Poirot, causing him to sneeze violently into a raised flipper. I'd never known him to sneeze, so I commented on it.

"Of course I sneezed, Hastings. You would, too, with this feather duster in your face."

The ostrich bent its long neck around until its huge eyes and large beak were inches from my face. It lowered its head on its snake-like neck to my height, for it was a few inches taller than me.

"Feather duster?" It said, emphasizing each of the four syllables.

"Sir, my apologies, I…"

"Sir?"

"Madam?" I stammered, not sure how one determined the sex of an ostrich or any other bird for that matter. (*I had no confirmation for Poirot's gender, assuming that whomever had given him a male name, knew what they were doing. Perhaps it was his self-assuredness when he had no right to it that caused me not to question.*) She hadn't noticed Poirot, so I didn't correct the misapprehension of the source for the feather duster insult. This made me feel a bit heroic because I was staring into a rather dangerous-looking beak behind which two enormous eyes stared at me, unblinking.

"The point is," I said, straightening to as full a height as I could muster, "I sincerely apologize for any perceived insult."

"Cindy?" a voice chimed from somewhere to my left, and the giant bird and I were released from our staring competition as Cindy spun to our left, once again dusting the top of Poirot's head with her ample plumage.

Poirot sneezed, and this caused Cindy to stop; her snake-like neck craned (*I'm just realizing that is a mixed chimeric metaphor, my apologies*) backward, and she looked down.

"Oh, what have we here?"

"We have," Poirot replied, "Poirot."

"A penguin," another voice intruded. It was the same man who'd called out to Cindy, and he joined us. He was a stout, red-faced man wearing slacks and a brown checked sports coat with western-style suede yoke and panels. Under that, he wore a white polo shirt buttoned to the top and a string tie bearing a large chunk of turquoise set in ornate silver. I looked down to confirm my suspicion that snake-skin cowboy boots might complete the ensemble. From his dress, I thought he was a Texan, but I perceived an Australian accent when he spoke.

"Welcome, Poirot penguin," he said, bending to extend a hand for Poirot to shake—a custom that my friend disliked participating in only slightly less than hugging. I broke in and introduced myself, shaking the man's outstretched hand, then begged for a moment to sign in and retrieve our name tags. When I looked up again, Cindy had wandered down the hall and pecked at a drinking fountain outside the lavatory doors. She would hit the button to make the water flow, then try to drink as it shut off. This was repeated several times.

"Hastings, you say? And Mr. Poirot. Great to meet you. Name's Pettigrew, Forrest Pettigrew. I'm doing a bit on the Yowies. Hope you'll join us." He pointed to one of the doors—Room four.

"I'm afraid I may have offended your friend." Down the hall, a kind passerby held the fountain's button for the poor creature so it could drink. "The aborigines used ostrich eggs as water canteens, didn't they?"

"No, mate, everyone gets that wrong. Them were emu eggs. Ostriches didn't arrive in wild breeding flocks until the 70s when some asshole let a few loose. Cindy, here's a descendant from one of them. Now, if they'd just eat the damn Cane toads, it'd settle the score."

I felt a bit the fool.

"I have ideas about your Yowies," Poirot spoke up.

"Do ya now?" Pettigrew said, rubbing his chin, clearly amused. "Maybe after my talk, *Yowie or Bunyip? Cryptid or Spirit?* Same title as my latest book." He pointed to a table of books down the hall where books and pamphlets by the presenters were laid out for sale. Pettigrew gave us a little half salute, turned, and, collecting Cindy, entered Room Four.

A decent crowd of, I'd say, sixty attended. I struggled to sit through Mr. Pettigrew's lecture. He used PowerPoints and fuzzy nighttime video clips. The videos showed Pettigrew and his team camping in Australia's outback, filming rustling branches and vague shadows in the dark of night while scaring each other with, "What's that?" "Did you see that?" Poirot, however, was on the edge of his seat (Quite literally as conference seating did not anticipate penguins.)

After the presentation, Poirot tried to talk Pettigrew into presenting his giant penguin theories. Pettigrew hurriedly escaped to the book table, where a line of people awaited his autograph. There were, I noted, five books he was selling and signing. How anyone could squeeze more than a single page of output from the meager content I'd seen presented confounded me. He periodically shook out his busy pen hand to grasp proffered hands. Cindy collapsed her long legs and sat on the floor by his side, head bobbing up to examine each fan as they talked to Pettigrew. I didn't think we'd have a chance to speak to him at length, so after assuring Poirot we'd likely find the fellow at the hotel bar after the conference, we wandered over to the next session.

I found one empty seat for Poirot just in front of the podium—even standing on a chair, his sightline would have been blocked otherwise. Other seats filled quickly, so I stood near the front with my back to the wall where I could keep an eye on Poirot.

"Will you be comfortable?" Poirot asked, "I need not be guarded if you wish a seat elsewhere?"

I assured him that I was fine and needed a break from sitting. Also, I rather enjoyed my vantage point, from where I could observe audience members. I'd guess eighty chairs had been set up, and they were almost all filled. The aisle down the center reminded me of a wedding—one set of family and friends on the left and the others on the right. I wondered if the believers and non-believers in the room could be divided similarly and if one side would have far more people than the other. There was a movie screen at the front of the room, as we'd had in the last lecture, and someone, I assumed was a technician for the venue, was at the room's podium. After a moment, the ceiling projector came on, displaying a title screen. "Bigfoot in the British Isles: Ape or Wildman?" I considered that an overly binary choice.

Standing on his chair seat, Poirot began subtly marching in place, going back and forth like a bowling pin that had just been grazed—he did that when he was excited.

The door to my right opened, and I had to take a half-step back as two men entered. One was young, athletic, and fresh-faced, the other older, bald, and with a closely trimmed, full-faced beard. The person I'd assumed was simply a technician turned out to be one of the conference organizers. She went to the podium and made introductions. The young man, Spencer Crywood, represented Cryptozoology's new wave and would present the Wildman hypothesis. He was, by trade, a medical imaging specialist (aka x-ray tech.) The other, older man, Robert Baker, represented the more traditional Bigfoot school of thought. He was a mechanical engineer of some type. Both would be signing books and DVDs for sale after the lecture. Applause greeted each upon introduction. These were known entities in this world.

I found myself more interested than I'd anticipated, which was a low bar as I expected to be bored silly. The younger of the two, Spencer, went first, cataloging how the Wildman motif stretched back throughout all of European history. The many stories from many lands and times struck me as persuasive, and I thought this was perhaps based on something actual. Not to out-speculate Poirot, but I had to wonder if it was more plausible that surviving Neanderthals explained the encounters. Indeed, I felt this was a more likely narrative than Poirot's giant penguins. As if reading my mind, Spencer next introduced the very idea: what if these were surviving Neanderthals? Appropriate PowerPoint slides went up— one showing a timeline of when humans and Neanderthals occupied Europe simultaneously.

"Just ten years ago, the same *experts*," he spat out the word experts, "would have told us the two had no association whatsoever. Notice how close the words *anthropologist* and *apologist* sound." This drew laughs from the crowd.

The idea that Neanderthals or some other extinct line of humans might account for Wildman sightings appealed to me, perhaps because I'd thought of it independently only seconds earlier. This argument seemed to erode the Bigfoot hypothesis, and when he was done, he turned the podium over to the other fellow, Robert Baker.

Baker returned to the original title screen, reminding

the audience that he and Spencer represented the two sides of the Bigfoot/Wildman hypothesis. Like professional wrestlers, I expected to see them drinking together in the bar later, no matter how heated the public argument became. He, too, had slides showing his prime suspect, an ape called Gigantapithicus. He also had fuzzy videos of shadows among the trees. Drawn outlines reinforced, or perhaps created the idea that the images were of a large ape-like creature. Next came the science.

"These are the dates from the *official* timeline of its extinction." He said the word *official* with the same venom his partner had spat out the word *expert.*

He pointed to the screen.

*Gigantopithecus Blacki became extinct 300,000 years ago.*

"300,000 years ago? Yet, just last year, a man saw a Bigfoot from a train whilst traveling from Exeter to Bristol Temple Meads. And they've been seen in the South Downs and also in Harting Down in West Sussex."

Though I'd nearly failed my undergraduate Formal Logic course, I'd have felt confident in challenging that. The presentation went on in like manner, with the two going back and forth with battling conjectures. Poirot, for his part, became increasingly agitated to the point of occasionally raising a flipper, yet he remained polite. But as soon as they asked for questions, he raised a flipper and asked to be heard.

"Oh," remarked Spencer, who was the one promoting the Wildman hypothesis. (*I use the term loosely as neither of them had hypothesized, in the formal sense.*) "I've been watching you, and you seem quite interested. Is it because perhaps you've seen a creature?"

Poirot started to speak, but the other presenter said, "We need to get a microphone to you. Anyone with questions, please wait until someone comes with the microphone." The woman who'd set up the equipment produced such a device, walked over, and thrust it at Poirot.

"Ack!" Poirot said, in surprise. He regained composure and spoke into the proffered mic, "Witnesses describe encounters with a large upright, bipedal animal. Why do you assume it must be either a human or an ape? Have you not heard of the *Kumimanu biceae* or the more recent *Kairuku waewaeroa*, better known as the Colossus penguin? This was a creature that stood over seven feet tall and who perhaps ruled the ancient world during the last Ice Age with a lost civilization in Antarctica, now buried under miles of ice."

"Um…?" Spencer blinked, mouth agape. When he regained his composure, he said, "A penguin. You're suggesting Bigfoot is a penguin?"

The bald one stepped up to the podium to use the microphone. "Spence, I think we should ask if anyone else has any questions." He nodded to the woman with the mic, who stepped back from Poirot. "Any questions on our presentation?" she asked.

Several people had raised hands. She pointed at a large man near the back of the room, as far from Poirot as possible.

"Yes," the man said once the microphone had made its way to him. "I'm interested in this giant penguin thing. I'd never heard of it." There was a murmur of assent from the crowd.

"A lost civilization of giant penguins in Antarctica!" the man next to him said, loud enough to be picked up on the mic. More excited voices chimed in.

I saw our friend from earlier, Forrest Pettigrew, the Australian who had done the Yowie presentation, and his ostrich, Cindy, standing at the back near the door.

"Oy! Hold up!" he yelled, and perhaps it was his

Australian accent, but everyone shut up. The woman with the mic brought it over, and Pettigrew plucked it from her hand. "I don't know, but we've never got a good look at the Yowies. Maybe we are stuck on it being an ape because we're apes."

"Why not some bird?" Cindy said, snaking her beak to the mic. She waved her head around and made throat-clearing sounds.

The bald man at the podium tapped his microphone. "Can we get back to the topic?"

Another man took the mic from Pettigrew and spoke into it. "You know, I just read that they found a pyramid in Antarctica with LiDAR. Could that be from this lost giant penguin civilization?"

Loud chatter filled the room, and people began arguing with one another. When someone yelled out, demanding, "What about these penguins?" it became clear that the two presenters had lost the crowd. I thought it best to leave. As we left, Poirot was accosted by several people demanding to know more. In the space of five minutes, the myth of *The Lost Antarctic Empire of the Giant Penguins* was birthed before me.

# CHAPTER EIGHT

## POIROT AND THE LOST ANTARCTIC EMPIRE OF THE GIANT PENGUINS

After attending a presentation at a cryptozoological conference, Poirot became obsessed with his crackpot theory, which states that Bigfoot could be explained as sightings of an extinct giant species of penguins. I'll be harsh in my assessment, having been present at its conception. His theory was a dog's dinner of extinct penguins, fantasies about Antarctica, and ideas shouted out by run-amok attendees at the end of a Bigfoot lecture we'd attended. Poirot then macheted a path through a jungle of disconnected facts, forgetting that it was he who had made the thing up, swallowing it whole like one of his tasty mackerels from Ellis and Jones Fishmongers.

It did not stop there.

After seeing the vigorous book sales and the attendants fawning over their authors at the conference, he set out to write a book of his own.

Despite our friendship, this somewhat irked me on two points: one, his theory was rubbish bordering on codswallop, and two, because a penguin's arm appendages are rather bony, fused, and solid affairs. So, unless I wished to suffer frequent keyboard replacements, it left the typing to me.

An Australian fellow we'd met at the Cryptozoological conference who'd written several books on the Yowie (Australia's answer to Bigfoot) connected Poirot to his publisher. Thereafter, it became a bit of a dash because once the word got out, William Spinacre's talent manager, Lady Gilderd Freist-Forstcrindle, began pressing Poirot for an appearance on *The Report with William Spinacre* to discuss the upcoming book. That would make Poirot's third guest appearance on that popular interview show. Frankly, the offer from the show surprised me after Poirot's last visit, when his detective associates, a pack of monkeys, had caused considerable distress.

Thankfully, my typing tasks were less than I'd feared because Poirot had developed the average undergraduate's skill of cutting and pasting passages gleaned from numerous pseudoscientific websites. I warned of plagiarism, and he solved that, in his mind, by exchanging a few adverbs and adjectives here and there. Similarly, appropriated photos and images took up many other pages. These he titled with leading questions. For example, he wrote below a side-by-side photo of two cave openings:

*Is this cave in Argentina the rumored entrance to a tunnel leading to the opening (on the right) in Antarctica?*

The image on the left was a cave that could have been anywhere in the world. The image on the right was of a cave opening that could be any icebound place on the planet.

Pictures and all, he managed to stretch out his book: *The Lost Antarctic Empire of the Giant Penguins* subtitled *Bigfoot, Solved?* to a respectable two-hundred and ninety pages when printed. It drifted off course a bit, covering various arcana of Antarctica: Admiral Bird's secret diary, hidden UFO bases, hollow Earth theories, and of course, Nazis. To add anything to this over-rich mélange would be an accomplishment, so I have to give it to Poirot for being the first to add a lost civilization of giant penguins. During this time, Poirot continued his frequent visits with our upstairs neighbor, Clive. The benefit of this for me was that, during this time, Clive seemed less inclined to his habit of hovering like a gnat in our building's entrance, where he would use his considerable height to crane, giraffe-like, (*sorry for the mixed metaphorical phyla!*) over my shoulder as I retrieved my mail. I did not snoop on Poirot nor monitor his comings and goings, but I knew something significant was happening when I thought I spotted Spencer Crywood pressing the lift for Clive's floor. Crywood was the young English bigfoot hunter we had met at the Bigfoot conference. I noted Poirot's suspicious absence that afternoon and queried him on this later, asking if it was indeed Crywood I'd seen. He apologized for being unable to tell me, as he did not wish to *ruin the experiment.* Given the questionable legality of his past exploits, that caused me no small anxiety. Other strange characters came and went, sometimes carrying bundles when they visited Poirot in his room and sometimes they would all go upstairs to Clive's apartment.

I had wanted to spy, if I must confess. But I had my work, which I've previously explained (or failed to explain) as being somewhat but only partially within the actuarial finance and insurance fields, which takes me out of the country for days at a time. My life as a grey-suited number-cruncher assessing hedge risk factors in multi-billion-dollar corporate acquisition contracts makes my association with my odd little penguin friend a welcome respite. As it was, I only learned of the scheme as it unfolded. When I returned, I saw none of the earlier suspicious activity and even had a respite from Clive. Then, on the morning of my fourth day back:

"Come, Hastings," Poirot said. "The game is afoot. Dress for the moors and bring a change of clothes; we'll be spending the night. Our train leaves in an hour and forty minutes."

I had completed my morning ablations yet was still in my dressing gown.

"Must we?" I said, looking longingly at my half-consumed coffee.

"Yes, yes, Hastings. The others were up before dawn and are already in place. We must not tarry. We shall meet young Crywood and Robert Baker later at our destination." Baker was the older English bigfoot hunter who'd shared the lectern with Crywood at the Cryptozoological conference.

Per Poirot's instructions, we took a taxi to Charing Cross Station, where I learned our destination was neither the hills nor some foggy moor (as my attire aimed at) but rather Tunbridge Wells. Tunbridge Wells is—for my non-British readers—how shall I describe it? Once the location of King James' hunting lodge, today, the town of Tunbridge Wells is not where adventures sprout but where adventurers go to retire. In literature, anyway. It was where James Bond and his new bride, Tracy Di Vincenzo, wished to live in marital bliss, and, in the movie Lawrence of Arabia, a friend of T.E. Lawrence's yearned to settle there after living through the Arab Revolt. A satirical television show portrayed a farcical revolution in Tunbridge Wells with the slogan, "Liberty, Equality, Gardening." If you now understand that Tunbridge Wells is a mediocre bedroom community where nothing significant, let alone startling, has ever or will ever occur, I have done my job. It is an hour's train ride from London, and over two hundred train trips shuttle back and forth daily. Considering giant penguins, Tunbridge Wells is as far from Antarctica as possible, thus lacking any such expansive romantic possibilities. (*Checking a globe—the polar opposite, or antipode of Tunbridge Wells is somewhere within the Waitangi, Chatham Islands, New Zealand.*)

On our train ride, I expressed my doubts. However, Poirot claimed that there had been reported instances of a large cryptid in the commons over the past few days and that Crywood had gone there to check on those reports. I admit there is considerable wilderness in its two-hundred-acre commons and surrounding farmland where—given sufficient imagination—a giant creature could skulk about.

Poirot further claimed that encounters with large bipedal cryptids had been reported with some regularity over the past seventy years or so. The latest was in 2012 when a dog walker startled a creature who roared at him (and presumably his dog) and then disappeared into the woods after making his objection to their presence clear. Another reported instance had a large creature breaking off a tree branch and using it as a toothpick. I've mentioned the acres of woodland in the Tunbridge Wells Commons. Still, it had a busy road running through it, contained a regulation Cricket field, was crisscrossed with bike and jogging paths, and was surrounded by suburbs and vacation lodges—not what you or I would deem cryptid-friendly territory. I'd been there, from time to time, in my youth and recalled asphalt bike trails and narrow footpaths, often through dense woodlands. A feature popular with rock climbers was an eight-acre area of large sandstone boulders called High Rocks.

As for myself, I was looking forward to our visit to Mount Edgcumbe—a bed and breakfast where Crywood was staying—as it had a fine restaurant and pub. How the inn got the name is up for debate, but being only a hundred feet above the surrounding land, it's not for its elevation. As mentioned, there were access roads and paved trails, but I could not imagine how Crywood planned for Poirot to get around in the generally rugged terrain of the commons—where one might expect to observe an elusive creature.

While on the train, I used my phone to refresh my memory of Mount Edgcumbe's menu. So, after getting off the train, I imagined lunch for our little group: Duck Spring Rolls for Crywood, Baker, and myself, and the array of seafood options for Poirot—anything from the Prawn and Crayfish cocktail to the Seafood Board featuring Smoked Salmon, Squid, Whitebait, and, of course, an irresistible Mackerel Pâté.

In the hotel lobby, Crywood greeted us with the same youthful enthusiasm I recalled from his talk at the Cryptozoology conference. He had a bag of camera equipment and was dressed as one might if hiking the Alps. He informed us that Baker had called him and, coming from a longer distance, had decided to meet us after lunch rather than rush his morning.

After checking in, Crywood, Poirot, and I proceeded to the hotel's large patio overlooking a broad meadow below. When dining with Poirot, this arrangement—patio dining—was one I found required the least amount of disagreeable negotiation with a restaurant's management. I appreciated the difficulty they faced—without offending guests—determining the difference between pets, service animals, and voiced animals.

Most of the six or so tables were occupied, and a couple of voiced creatures were seated at other tables when we arrived—I could usually tell a voiced animal in a blink. There were just as many these days, despite my cousin Averill's aggressive campaign against the conversion that gave voice to an animal's inner thoughts—it turned out they had many. A voiced Pug was speaking out of my earshot but must have been at the end of some punchline because his human table mates suddenly erupted into laughter. The other voiced animal, a Capibara, the docile semi-aquatic rodent the size of a sheep, sat at the table next to us, along with a middle-aged woman. She wore a white tea dress and a broad sunhat—the Capibara, not the woman—and was munching on a vegetable spring roll. The Capibara does not seem far down a direct Darwinian line from a tree stump—the progression being, tree stump, to floating log, to Capibara. In its native habitat—Northeastern South America—it's known as nature's park bench because other animals—from monkeys to birds—find its enormous head a convenient place to take a load off, as they say. I turned slightly to better hear what its woman companion was saying, and the topic seemed to be gossip concerning the Royal Family.

The Capibara listened and then held up a finger (it had four on each hand) to signal a pause. Then, after extensive chewing—its tiny lower jaw in its massive head working side to side—it replied in a surprisingly rich contralto expressing her disgust that there was a rumor that Princess Anne might be dying her hair. A short series of clicks and a sharp whistle followed this.

"Hastings?" It was Poirot. By his expression, I saw I had missed some key bit of dialog at my table.

"Young Crywood was outlining this afternoon's expedition."

Poirot's sobriquet, *Young Crywood,* struck me as humorous as, by my estimation, Poirot himself was barely four years old. Also, although Tunbridge Wells Commons was an extensively wooded area of over two hundred acres, referring to a walk-through as an *expedition* struck me as hubris, but I held my tongue. Before I could make my insincere apologies for missing the crucial, life-saving details of whatever daring trek they planned, a waiter appeared, and we gave our orders along predictable lines: the fish platter for Poirot, the duck spring rolls and pints of bitters for both Crywood and myself. (*I once worried about how Poirot might feel about me ordering duck, or any other avian meats, but he'd told me that my concerns were foolish and illogical as, no one ate penguins outside sharks, Orka, and Leopard seals and that he'd never seen penguin on the menu at any restaurant.*)

Having traversed these lands many times in my youth in various school outings, I knew the commons as nothing more than an extra-large playground and, in a recent visit, found nothing had changed. Given the stodgy British nature, I'd more expect New York's Central Park to change its landscaping.

Tunbridge Commons did have quite a varied terrain, so after hearing the post-prandial plan of venturing northward to an area about a mile away that I knew was especially wooded with narrow, sandy footpaths where two people could hardly walk side-by-side, I expressed my concern that by the time a penguin might waddle to the location, that it would be late evening and dark, or, depending on Poirot's determination or lack thereof, perhaps into the next day.

"Not a problem," Young Crywood (now Poirot had me saying it!) said with a slap on the table. "I've rented a pram. It will be waiting for us. I simply need to ask for it at the hotel desk. There's a rental place just up the A26, and they do good business with holiday seekers who have found they underestimated the extent of the common's grounds."

"A perambulator? You know what that is, don't you, Poirot?"

"Perambulator? Of course, my friend. One simply needs to take the word apart, examining its Latin roots. It is a means of making someone or something ambulatory. The word *ambulance* is an example. I shall be transported along the footpaths in comfort, safety, and style."

I don't think of myself as a particularly sadistic fellow,

nor one to engage in cruel jibes, but, in this case, I must confess that my own *imp of the perverse* made me still my face in a type of rigor mortis and say nothing at that moment, wishing to see Poirot's reaction when he found that Young Crywood intended for Poirot to submit to being wheeled to our designated location riding in a baby stroller.

We found Robert Baker, the English bigfoot hunter, waiting for us at the inn's lobby, where he'd just checked in and exchanged greetings.

"You could have lunched with us," Crywood said.

"I already feel this is a wild goose chase. I wasn't going to lose sleep. I mean, really, Crywood—Tunbridge Wells?"

"There's a surprising amount of wooded area here," Crywood said sheepishly.

Baker waved his room key card in the air. "Oh, come on, Spence. I'm only here because you said you had dramatic evidence, and a visit to the commons isn't the worst way to spend a day or so."

"You'll see," Crywood said.

Baker raised the handle on his suitcase. "Sorry, I find that hard to believe," he said over his shoulder as he walked toward the stairs.

I said nothing, wondering how anything qualifies as hard to believe for a man who has spent decades searching for Bigfoot in the British Isles.

Crywood set down his video equipment bag and excused himself to get the pram for Poirot. I waited, readying myself to produce a satisfying smirk when Poirot caught sight of the baby carriage. However, when Crywood reappeared, he was pushing a mobility scooter. It was a bit smaller than usual and controlled, including the steering, by one joystick.

"That's not a pram," I said, surprised.

"What else would one call it?" Crywood asked.

"A Rascal," Baker offered. "Or Gooter, you know: geriatric scooter?"

Tunbridge Wells was a popular location for tourists of all types, including those with mobility issues, so Crywood had no difficulty finding a local company, ABC Rentals, offering a variety of mobility scooters.

Poirot declared it an exemplary device for wheeled ambulation. I, of course, was crestfallen, expecting a baby carriage.

Crywood lifted Poirot onto the seat, and I was surprised Poirot offered no resistance. As far as my experience went, Poirot hated being picked up by anyone but myself, and that was restricted to what was necessary, such as being lifted into and out of the bathtub. I admit to having felt somewhat left out lately, what with all the visitors, the mysterious goings-on, and Poirot spending time at Clive's (whom I'd not seen since my return.)

Poirot attempted to master the joystick control of his chariot while the rest of the party played defense, protecting the hotel lobby's furniture and decorations. It took only a few minutes for the desk clerk to throw us out while simultaneously seeming exceedingly polite.

Our expedition continued outside. I can't say whether Poirot's abilities improved or if it was that there were fewer things to crash into. Soon, we set out on a trail to the west, parallel to Mount Ephraim Road, then north of the Mount Edgcumbe rock formation towards the upper cricket ground. The plan was to cross over and follow a part of the old two-mile horse racing course (now overgrown) to a wooded area near Fir Tree Pond. I found out on the way that it was near that pond where there had been reports of recent Bigfoot activities.

Poirot navigated the paths without too many

encounters with shrubbery—at one point declaring himself a natural, except for occasionally running into the backs of Baker's legs, whose creative expletives made me suspect a nautical past.

It was early autumn, and the groves of deciduous trees were turning from green to gold. (Besides that word, deciduous, the extent of my arboreal knowledge is knowing a maple from an oak because of the twirly things.)

The temperature was around twenty (or upper sixties for those across the pond.) I enjoyed the smell of the forest and the sound of birds—again, do not ask me the species. It struck me at that moment that while there was a categorical vocabulary—a labeling—hidden from me, my ignorance of the words did not diminish the wonderous sensations I experienced. It made me think of the voicing of animals. Did we really add much by giving them words to express their feelings?

My musings were interrupted by yet another string of expletives, this time from myself as Poirot piloted his scooter into my Achilles tendon, dislodging my shoe.

After an impromptu conference among the expedition participants, we decided to have Poirot take the lead with Crywood calling out directions—left or right—whenever we came to a branching of the path. That proved safest for all but the bordering shrubbery. Our fellow hikers and their pets we encountered succeeded in moving to safety due to Poirot's liberal use of his craft's beeper while yelling, "Make way! Make way!"

We halted our caravan at the aforementioned Fir Tree Pond. It was most definitely assigned the title of *pond* and not *lake*. It was algae-colored and less than fifty yards across. When I asked what species of bird I was hearing, Crywood informed me that it was frogs and not birds that were chirping. From examining a walking path map,

I knew that a road ran along the park's far side and, true to the pond's name, fir trees predominated the landscape. Insects buzzed, dragonflies and other winged creatures thankfully disinterested in human blood. I heard barking, followed by a man's voice hushing the dog. Off towards the tree line, a young couple with a toddler was sitting on a blanket, noshing cheese—I assume—and drinking white wine from plastic cups—the couple, not the toddler. The dog I'd heard was theirs. It was a Cocker spaniel or some other reddish-brown dog of the same size who accepted a treat from the man and lay down.

"Well?" Baker said. "It's early afternoon. Why are we here, Crywood?"

He meant, I learned, not why they were at that location but at what time of day. They had a heated discussion in which Baker claimed that Bigfoot was crepuscular. I learned that the word meant that Bigfoot, as with deer and other woodland creatures, liked to roam about in the hours of diminished sunlight—at dawn and dusk and that Baker was not objecting to the entire enterprise but rather the timing.

Seeing his Poirot's trepidatious attempts to get down from his scooter, like someone trying to find the top ladder rung while climbing down from the roof of a house, I offered to lift him off but he waved me off, deciding to stand up on the seat as it gave him a more commanding view of the field.

Crywood looked at his watch, then unpacked his camera from his bag. He continued his argument with Baker, saying he preferred daylight so that if something happened, he could obtain clear images as opposed to the typical unlit, shadowy shapes one sees on the internet.

The child with the family began calling, "*Mama, mama,*" and pointing to the shrubbery where branches were rustling. Crywood raised his camera and started recording. Baker said it was just the wind. I doubted this as the branches of a shrub at the base of one of the pine trees seemed rather more animated than the wind would account for.

Poirot cried out, "There. There! There it is!"

I saw no *there* there besides moving branches but felt a tingle of anticipation.

The little family rose, the father picking up the child and backing away from the tree line. Then we heard it: a deep howl followed by a whoop. It was certainly no animal I was familiar with. The dog began barking furiously but backed away into the clearing with its owners.

Although still bright daylight, anything in the woods was dark and shaded in contrast. I could only see a vague shape in that murky darkness. Whatever it was, caused the rustling of a fir tree branch seven or eight feet off the ground.

"Are you getting this, Crywood?" Baker called out.

"Yes, yes!" Crywood continued to aim his camera toward the commotion.

There was another howl, but this ended in coughing. I thought I heard a faint *damn* from the creature, then a continuation of the howl, followed by a *whoop!*

"Perhaps we can draw it out," Poirot said. By then, the little family had retreated to our position, holding their picnic blanket in front of them as a shield.

"What is it?" the woman asked.

"Bigfoot," said Baker. "My God, a perfect specimen."

The thing in question continued moving just beyond the tree and shrub line and remained mainly hidden in the darkness to our left.

"Perhaps we can persuade it to come closer," Poirot said. "Come out, come out!"

"Are you insane," Baker said, "They can tear a man in

two!"

"Come out, come out!" Poirot cried again.

The branches cracked under a terrible strain, and we saw something emerging from the forest. There was a bit of activity; then all went silent.

"I'm stuck!" a voice cried out.

A branch snapped, and now free, the creature stepped forward, half-falling into the open. To my utter shock, it was, for all purposes, a seven-foot-tall penguin.

They say that your entire life flashes before you at the moment of death. Being merely stunned; it was only the previous week that flashed before my eyes. It now made sense—Poirot sense, I grant you, but sense: the visitors carrying bundles traipsing up to Clive's flat; Poirot, declining to answer if Crywood was involved, telling me that he must not *ruin the experiment*; and, more telling, Clive's absence the past few days.

I looked upon the scene with new illumination.

The giant penguin, nee Clive, wobbled a bit, waving his flippers, calling out that *whoop, whoop,* vocalization.

The costume, I must say, was first-rate. Clive, if not seven feet tall, must have been near that. A clever costumer had somehow replicated the extinct Antarctic penguin—recently discovered—that Poirot had shown me artist recreations of, and Clive was the perfect human to inhabit such a costume. It rivaled anything that Jim Henson's studio created. It was dark brown with a white front and armed with a three or four-foot menacing beak. Think of Big Bird but with a sturdy neck—but it wasn't a happy, fluffy yellow mascot. Instead, it was a nightmare creature that would have frightened rather than amused. The child began screaming at the top of its little lungs, and the couple, passing the child back and forth between them, hastened their retreat while holding their blanket as a shield.

During this, Crywood continued filming. To his credit, Baker stood his ground, saying, "I see! I see!" repeatedly. Had I not put the proverbial two-and-two together, I don't know how brave I would have been in the situation. Poirot managed to stand up on the seat of his scooter. He was hopping and raising his flippers in triumph.

The little dog ran forward, emboldened by whatever good-sense-overriding humors nature provides canids for such situations. The dog's owner yelled (what I presume was its name and not a request for police assistance) *Copper! Copper!* But it was too late. The animal tore off towards his perceived enemy with what I thought was remarkable speed for a creature with such short legs.

Clive/Giant Penguin was moving slowly to his left, still hugging the perimeter of the tree line. I was unsure how well he could see from within his costume, but this question was resolved for me when I saw him step into the little pond. He must have felt the water seep into his right foot because he lifted it as much as possible while wearing a full-body penguin costume. His pose set him off-balance so that when Copper the dog closed the distance and leapt at him, Clive toppled like a felled tree into the shallow water with a splash.

One foot jutted out, and Cooper seized it in his fangs.

"Help! Help me," Clive yelled, somewhat muffled by the heavy costume. Copper pulled one of the faux penguin's feet free, backed onto the grass, and began shaking his prize as if it were a squirrel. While this ended the dog attack, there was still the problem that Clive, now waterlogged, could not right himself. Flailing and splashing, Clive attempted to roll, but slipping in the mud, he only made matters worse.

I shook myself, realizing that my group—Crywood, Baker, and Poirot—and I had been stunned into inaction.

We all seemed to awaken at once as though slapped. Poirot was at the forefront, beeping the horn on his scooter and setting off at top speed—a maximum of four MPH, but he had a bit of a head start due to the torque of his electric drive. I couldn't recall the last time I had to run and found my limbs responding sluggishly. Crywood, the youngest of us, sprinted ahead, quickly passing Poirot and the rest of us. Heedless of the cold and muck, he splashed into the pond and managed to lift at least the top part of Clive's costume above the water.

"Ack, I'm drowning." Clive's gagging voice was tinged with desperation.

Crywood dragged him halfway onto dry land, and I grabbed an exposed foot and pulled it. I fell backward, holding a wet sock. I heard a beeping and turned just in time to see Poirot fumbling at his controls. He ran his scooter full speed into the water, thankfully missing the others but raising a wake that further inundated Clive. Baker had a firm hold on the ankle, and between him and Crywood, they wrangled Clive, costume and all, to dry land.

Clive's muffled cries rang out. "Get this damnable thing off me."

Baker sat down from exhaustion. I dropped the wet sock I was holding and went to help Crywood, who was examining the costume for a zipper, or some means to extract Clive. It was covered in some sort of short fake fur with padding underneath. We pulled on the head portion, hoping it would come off, but to no avail. Poirot, high and dry, standing on the seat of his otherwise submerged scooter, called out instructions, but we could not find the fasteners he described because the fur was matted and covered with mud and algae. We removed the foot the dog had not pulled off, and while I held the head part by the beak, Crywood and Baker managed to pull Clive out of the bottom, accompanied by horrible squishing, wet, *schlopping* sounds. (It was somewhat like I imagined what seeing a live birth must be like and resolved never to witness such an event in reality.) Soon, Clive's head emerged, gasping for air. Thankfully, he was fully clothed in yoga pants and a tee shirt.

"Good God, Clive," I said.

Clive stood, a full-body shudder engulfing him as he rained water droplets on us like a dog.

"Ahem." Poirot stood imperiously upon the seat of his scooter like the captain on the deck of his sinking ship. "A little assistance?" he called out. Since I'd last looked, his vehicle had glided further into the pond, with only the chair now above the water.

"Fer God's sake, ya daft idjet," Baker called back, his northern accent showing in the excitement, "You're but ten feet from dry land… and you're a waterfowl. Swim for it."

I knew this was the wrong thing to say to Poirot. He responded by flapping his arms. "Waterfowl? Waterfowl? Poirot is no waterfowl!"

"Come, come, Poirot," I said in a soothing tone, "It's not like we have a life raft. Just jump off and swim."

"The muck," replied Poirot, gesturing to the waters below him.

"We'll hose you off back at the hotel," offered Crywood.

Again, not the right thing to say.

"Our room has a tub. I'll draw a bath for you." Both replied in the affirmative, with Clive begging Poirot to get on with it as he was cold, damp, and mucky himself.

"Just jump," I said, "It can't be above your head."

He did, and I found that I had sadly misjudged the depth. His head bobbed up, and he opened his beak with a *ghhhaa*, then he half swam, half waded to join us.

Crywood and Clive had been running this little scheme for a couple of days, and Crywood had a van/changing room parked on the road on the far side of the pond. With no rope to pull it out, we left the scooter in the pond and watched it sink slowly with the setting sun. I thought, there lies Poirot's book advance. Poirot waddled along with us to the van, complaining the entire time. I helped Poirot and Clive to the van, and we all got in. The enclosed space amplified just how awful our muddy duo smelled. I was grateful to pull up to the hotel and get some fresh air. Crywood and I distracted the desk clerk while Baker ushered Clive and Poirot to the stairs.

After going to our rooms and showering off pond muck and a bath for Poirot, we dressed and retired to the hotel's intimate bar, where they assured us we could order dinner. A friendly fire awaited us in a rustic stone fireplace. We seized a table next to it when a party of nuns, wearing traditional habits, were leaving. They gave Poirot admiring glances, and Poirot nodded politely in return. The entire room was walled, somehow in stone, like a cave. Bits of embedded mica sparkled as the firelight danced and flitted across the stone.

After we ordered, Crywood spoke. "Admit it, Baker, there was a moment you thought it was a Bigfoot."

"I don't have to admit a goddamn thing," he said loudly, then he looked sheepishly towards the retreating nuns covering the knuckles of one hand with the other, but the nuns were already through the door. "No, Crywood, I don't have to admit it. But you must concede that I was more a victim of a practical joke than a participant in a valid scientific experiment. My reaction proves what? That Bigfoot is an extinct giant penguin? A creature that died out millions of years ago yet somehow adapted to more temperate climes? It's…" he looked around and, seeing an elderly couple at a nearby table, blurted, "Poppycock!" (No doubt altering his first chosen expletive.)

"It is no mere conjecture, my friend," said Poirot, "as you shall see when my book is published."

Our drinks order arrived, and I sat back, sipping my stout, letting the fire warm me, listening to the back and forth, resisting all attempts to draw me to a side. I checked my watch, though I wasn't on a schedule. We could catch any number of trains back to London in the morning. Clive sipped an ale and looked over the dinner menu. I couldn't get much out of him except his assuring me that he was all right, followed by a brief shudder to belie that claim. The others jawed on—they may as well have been arguing about whether the Earth was flat or a cube. I pretended they were speaking in a foreign language and enjoyed the camaraderie. Poirot, Crywood, and Baker were fans of the same sport but for different teams, enjoying the same love of the game.

# CHAPTER NINE

## POIROT THE MEMSMERIST

The next few days were consumed with the fallout from our Tunbridge Wells adventure. The first issue was Clive. After nearly drowning while trapped in the giant penguin suit, Clive, while suffering no lasting physical issues, seemed psychologically affected. I should be thankful that he now avoided me in the hallway rather than being his usual overbearing self, but I could not help but be concerned.

The next matter was what to do with the giant penguin costume Clive had worn and nearly drowned in. I had deemed it a soggy, muddy, and stinking irredeemable mess and planned to toss it in the nearest bin, but Poirot insisted that we take it back on the train, having begged a couple of large trash bags from the hotel for that purpose. It was now at the cleaners, but I didn't share Poirot's high hopes. The import was that our Tunbridge debacle had gotten legs, or gone viral as they say, and Poirot was asked to appear for an upcoming segment on the television show, *The Report with William Spinacre.* The issue was the repairability of the suit. The plan was that, after the cleaners, it would go to the costumers who had initially made the thing. Poirot was confident it could be salvaged, whereas I wondered if it might be best that—like the ancient giant penguin order it was patterned after—it never waddled upon this earth again.

Lastly, there was the issue of responsibility for the ruined mobility scooter. Poirot claimed the crash into the pond was due to a faulty joystick controller. I contacted my attorney, cousin Averill for advice, and she demanded that we come to her office forthwith. Poirot took this as generosity, but he could stand to exhibit a tad more resistance to the effects of attention and flattery. I suspected Averill of having hidden machinations. She'd previously sought to push Poirot forward as the poster child for her talking animal rights crusade. I decided to go alone, after elevenses, for an initial meeting to ensure her concerns were limited to the scooter.

I prepared tea and set it out in the living room, and Poirot, sensing the time or hearing the clinking china, exited his room and joined me. I asked if any progress had been made on the costume, but the costume was not the only hurdle. Poirot had yet to convince our neighbor, Clive, to repeat his role. The suit was custom-fitted to Clive's excessively tall frame, but nearly drowning in the costume in a cold, mucky pond, Clive was loath to do it again. Poirot was confident in his powers of persuasion, whereas I felt we should prepare an alternate plan.

To gauge Clive's height, I once eyed him against the elevator frame one day and returned later with a tape. I measured just under seven feet. Somewhat familiar with statistics due to my occupation, which I've explained before as working with derivative risk assessment for those insuring against derivative insurance risks, I called upon my regular sources and learned that there were probably fewer than three thousand people—men—in the entire world at seven feet or taller. I realized I must have misjudged the mark, or it was an error due to parallax, but Clive was exceptionally tall.

I asked Poirot how tall Clive was as he had been involved in manufacturing the costume.

"How tall?" Poirot restated. "I see where you are heading with this line of questioning." I held myself back from pointing out that one question was hardly a line.

"You are implying that I cannot persuade Clive in time for my scheduled appearance. Which means you doubt my persuasive abilities."

"Only in this case," I replied and recommended placing an ad for someone as a standby, perhaps a visiting American basketball player.

"No need," Poirot said, taking a piece of Ojingeochae (dried julienned squid) from a plate. I was happy to find the Ojingeochae at a Korean market as it gave Poirot a snack at tea, as penguins don't eat biscuits. Poirot often commented on the uselessness of my eating non-nutritional items. My favorites, Jammie Dodgers, Custard Creams, and Jaffa Cakes, were hardly innocent of that criticism, particularly in that they came in brightly colored packets one might see disgorged from a vending machine. Being the only one in the house consuming such delicacies, I depended on individual packaging to keep them fresh. The Jaffa Cakes, in particular, have an interesting story that I'll skip the details on, assuming the reader's lack of interest in tax accountancy. But the issue spent years in the courts deciding if the small round flat treats were cakes, or biscuits—the government tax on cake being substantially less than biscuits.

Ah, but tea—Poirot enjoyed tea immensely. I noted that the relatively minor dose of caffeine in a cup sometimes overstimulated my diminutive friend. To be blunt, it often got him going off on rants. Therefore, I served him in a diminutive two-eared vintage cup— manufactured by Booth's of England. It had cost me a pretty penny at an antique stall, but Poirot could manage it easily with his flippers.

"No need," he repeated after chewing a morsel and taking a sip of tea. "I've been researching the particular form of claustrophobia afflicting Clive. Claustrophobia is the illusionary sense that one is trapped."

"But, Poirot," I objected. "He *was* trapped. It was no illusionary sense."

"Nevertheless, Hastings, there are techniques to employ—forms of hypnosis, eye movements, tapping… I've been researching."

"Eye movements? Tapping?" I'm sure I sighed at that because Poirot's notion of research was watching internet videos.

"Tapping." He tapped the coffee table three times in front of him rapidly. "Tapping. Thus. But on Clive, in selective spots."

"While he makes eye movements?"

"Yes, Hastings. Eye movements, up, down, left, right. The order and duration depend on the type of trauma. The subject follows these directions while imagining their worst fears."

"His worst fear would be drowning in a muddy pond in a park in Tunbridge Wells while trapped in a soggy penguin costume. Is that eyes up/down or left/right?"

Poirot set down his teacup. "You mock me, sir."

"Knowing how much your appearance on Spinacre's show means to you, I simply wish you'd consider alternatives. I'd volunteer, but Clive has a good foot on me—the costume would look absurdly baggy."

"Hasting, you would not volunteer even if it fit you."

"You have the measure of me there—not to make a pun."

For Clive's sake, I could only hope that they'd find that the costume would fail to be salvageable.

For my part, I set off for Cousin Averill's office. Poirot went to visit Clive, one floor above where Clive was house-sitting for his rather eccentric aunt. She was who-knew-where doing who-knew-what. Poirot said he noted a book or two on hypnosis in her odd book collection, which he hoped to peruse for tips on persuading Clive. This would have sponsored some reproval from me had I thought there was any chance that Poirot had the ability to put anyone asleep outside the recitations of his bespoke versions of Romantic period poetry.

Averill's spacious and well-appointed office reflected her success as a barrister. Personal achievements— medals and plaques from marathons and triathlons from around the world stood in well-lit bookcase shelves where, a dozen years earlier, law compendiums (now more easily searched digitally) might have impressed visitors.

I sought to get to the heart of the matter by handing her a copy of the demand letter from ABC Rentals of Tunbridge Wells. I said that it was true that Poirot had been driving the scooter in question when it was rendered inoperable.

She snatched the document from me, glanced at it, and blew air from pursed lips like a tank releasing pressure.

"Oh, Limpy, the demand is for the person who rented the thing, one Spencer Crywood," she whacked the paper with a manicured finger where Crywood had signed it.

"I know, but he's..." I didn't want to say someone of poor financial means as it would sound like I was asking her to extend charity.

"He's what? Non-compos mentis?"

"No, he's... he's a British Bigfoot hunter."

"So, the same."

"No, I mean, the poor fellow—nice young chap—has no real occupation and is of low financial means. Look, it was Poirot's fault, and I thought of the earlier situation about trespassing." Poirot had planned to board a boat without permission from the owners that tied up at the

Chelsea pier in hopes of finding stolen goods. Averill had explained that a penguin—talking or not—was no more liable for trespass than a seagull who might land on the mast. She'd wanted to press the matter. She even offered her services to the gang of burglars if they would pursue the claim of illegal discovery. But the gang decided their troubles with Scotland Yard were best solved by full confessions rather than becoming part of Averill's crusade to force a determination under the law concerning the status of talking animals.

She argued then that while past law could find that an animal's owner might be responsible for property damage, the animal could not be. Poirot (in common with wild animals) had no owner. Therefore, to claim that Poirot was responsible for the scooter, they had to classify Poirot as a human under the law. Averill may have agreed to look at the case as a way to force the law to recognize the legal personhood of talking animals. I admit to playing her as the purpose of my visit was that I believed that once ABC Rentals of Tunbridge Mills saw a challenge with her firm's prestigious letterhead, they'd drop the matter. Not to ruin the suspense, but this later turned out to be the case, leaving Averill rather miffed with me and me wondering when a vengeful strike would be coming. As I exited that meeting, my cell rang.

I went to answer, reasoning that only my office had my number. But, to my unwelcome surprise, I saw that the caller was my upstairs neighbor, Clive. Some time ago, he'd misplaced his phone, and Poirot pressured me to call to help locate it, which left my number on Clive's phone. Since then, I'd been dreading his call on my private cell phone. And now, here it was. I was headed home, so I decided to see what he wanted in person rather than be one of those obnoxious people screeching a one-sided conversation into their phones in public. A few minutes later, the phone rang again. I ignored it. I flagged a cab rather than wait for a bus. My phone rang again. I declined the call so I could communicate with the cabbie.

Seated and on the way, I saw a voicemail—to listen or not? I listened.

"It's Clive! (surprise) Something's happened to Poirot. I don't know what to do. Do I call a veterinarian or a GP—you know, because he's more human and talks? Do vets treat penguins anyway? I suppose they treat parrots who also talk… but Poirot isn't talking at the moment."

*Poirot not talking? It must be serious.*

I ended the message and told the driver to step on it. He pointed at the traffic ahead and said, "Sure, mate, I'll just engage the laser beam and cut a path."

Ignoring the insolence, I started to call my GP, but I didn't know what to tell her concerning Poirot's condition. Judging that I had another twenty minutes in traffic, I called Clive back. It rang and rang, and no one picked up. I tried several times, each time becoming more worried about Poirot.

By the time I got to my building, I was a wreck. I paid, exited the cab, and ran up to the front door which flung open with Clive standing behind it.

"Why didn't you answer," I asked.

"Answer? What? What?" Clive said, searching his pockets. "Oh, the phone must be upstairs."

"What's wrong with Poirot? Should I call an ambulance?" I asked, holding up my phone.

"No, no. It's hard to explain. Quick!" With that, he just released the door and spun around. I grabbed the closing door before it could latch and followed. He entered the elevator, and I caught the doors before they closed as he punched the button for his floor.

"Clive?" I said, hoping to prompt an explanation, but

he just stared at the doors, wringing his hands and breathing in little puffs like a toy locomotive.

When the elevator doors opened, Clive strode down the hall to his flat. He kicked aside the shoe he'd used to keep the door from closing and entered.

"Where is he?" I asked, looking around as I followed him inside.

"Here. Here." Clive led me to a door that turned out to be a bedroom—his absent aunt's bedroom, as it turned out.

I stepped inside, and there, standing before a long, free-standing wood-framed mirror, was Poirot. I'd seen him many times in this self-admiring pose in front of the long mirror in his room, but here, he lacked any animation—the head-turning admiration of his colorful beak and the general posturing. Here was a frozen penguin—he could have been a museum exhibit.

I've proven time and again, in my adventures with Poirot, that I lack the investigative detective gene, but I was able to assemble the visible clues, rapidly deducing what had occurred. Laying open, spine up on the nearest corner of the bed was a book entitled, "Self-Hypnosis: Your Key to a Better Life."

As a youth, I had the experience of hypnotizing chickens. I'd seen this done at Aunt G's farm (where a goat had attacked me, and Cousin Averill cruelly gave me the nickname Limpy). You hold the subject's beak to the ground and draw a straight line out from the beak or draw a circle around the poor creature. You can also draw a line with your finger from its wattles to its belly, hold its head under its wing like it's sleeping, or stare it down (although that can also promote an attack, as I found, much to Averill's amusement.) Most methods worked, and when you let go, the chicken remained in a sort of unmoving fugue state. Averill never tired of demonstrating this, at one point lining up a good six or so paralyzed victims. Being a few years my senior, and I, not having entered my growth spurt, she had tried it on me, wrestling me to the ground in the driveway and using the chalk we had for hopscotch to try various geometric patterns to attempt hypnosis. After several attempts, I pretended to be hypnotized to get her to stop. An infinity symbol was the last thing she'd drawn, and she put much mystical significance in that—she has a necklace with that symbol and swears it helps her sway judges and juries and to get people to do what she wants. I hadn't the heart to tell her the symbol was a coincidence because I'd run out of patience.

But here was Poirot, frozen like a hypnotized chicken—a comparison I knew I could never share with him without causing grave offense.

According to Clive, Poirot had been in this state for almost three hours. I considered clapping loudly, like we did to awaken the chickens. Then, I felt it might be a good idea to pick up the book and look at the pages he'd been reading for a possible solution. The page open on the right side seemed to be a self-hypnosis script with the aim of building greater self-confidence. It advised sitting in a quiet place, breathing slowly, and reminding yourself how loved you are by the entire universe and that sort of sentiment. I hadn't finished much of that dreck when I stopped and asked Clive, "Clive, why—I should say I have two questions: first, why self-hypnosis? I thought Poirot intended to employ tapping and mesmerism to relieve you of your fear of being trapped in the costume."

"Well, I…" Clive started.

"And the second question is, why did Poirot use this on himself? Wasn't Poirot seeking to muddle your brain and not his own? By muddle, I mean no offense but rather put you in some malleable state, open to suggestion."

"We did try the tapping, as well as attempting to hypnotize me. I'm afraid I'm not a good subject, or at least, that's what Poirot told me."

"So, it wasn't his lack of skill, I take it."

"Oh, no, no, he assured me it was not. Rather, some rare condition of my medulla, something, perhaps due to a childhood head injury or high fever."

"Medulla oblongata?"

"That's the sound of it. So, he said the only option would be for me to hypnotize myself. We'd found this book on the shelf among my aunt's books. I had reservations, so he bade me watch as he demonstrated how harmless it was."

"And, the mirror, I suppose, was his idea?" Knowing a mirror was always a tempting prop for Poirot.

"He said it was so I could observe his powerful self-hypnosis technique even as Persius had watched the Gorgon Medusa in the reflection of his polished shield without himself turning to stone."

"He said that?"

"I don't think he was comparing himself to a monstrous snake-haired creature—it was more the evocation of power—warning me to stay safe."

"But then it was he who turned to stone," I mused aloud.

"Quite." He sighed, then asked, "What shall we do?"

I thought of the chickens. If we let them be for a bit, they'd snap out of it—maybe in ten minutes or so, but Poirot had been at this for hours. We could also awaken a chicken with a clap and a yell. I worried that might cause harm, like waking a sleepwalker, if that urban legend was true. I wondered if the mirror was the key to the thing. Examining it, I saw that the large, oblong, oval-shaped mirror was suspended in a U-shaped holder and could flip end to end. I rocked it an inch and saw Poirot's gaze following the motion—up and down. With that premise established, I went for it, as they say. I flipped the bottom up and over, and as Poirot followed in his sight, he raised his beak so high he fell over backward.

Poirot gave out a rasping cough. I was worried he'd choke, but he called out, "Who put the ceiling on the wall?"

"You're simply disoriented, my dear friend," I said. "Don't rush things. It will soon come clear in a minute. Can I help you up?"

Eyeing me from his prone position, he said, "Up? It is you, Hastings, who needs set right, or has gravity finally given Newton the kick in the pants he's so long deserved?"

I was relieved that Poirot was unharmed and reasoned that he'd resolve the disorientation in his own time. "Clive, let's go to your kitchen and get us all a cuppa while we give the world time to right itself."

# CHAPTER TEN

## THE RETURN OF THE BEAST OF TUNBRIDGE WELLS

The cleaners and costumers had refurbished the giant penguin suit well before Poirot's guest spot on the William Spinacre show. It was in good shape, as was its intended wearer, our upstairs neighbor, Clive. The week before, Clive had hyperventilated at the mere thought of donning the great bulky thing. I was puzzled by his newfound courage. It certainly wasn't due to Poirot's attempts at calming him using hypnosis and various "new age" tricks he'd seen on the internet. Clive had proven the proverbial tough nut to crack, and my penguin friend only managed to hypnotize himself while standing in front of a mirror. Now, Clive was putting on the costume. He'd invited us up to his flat to help him perfect his act and select the most realistic or, in many cases, terrifying poses.

I say terrifying because, unlike my three-and-a-half-foot King penguin friend, the ancient giant penguin of 60 million years ago weighed as much as 350 pounds and stood at six or seven

feet. I can hardly imagine confronting one as I found the costume rather intimidating when looming over me in tight quarters. I understand that Sesame Street's Big Bird was over eight feet tall—the head and beak above the actor's height. Still, being bright yellow and feathery with the voice of angelic kindliness, I could never imagine Big Bird's two-foot beak as a pointed instrument of death (though I suppose he could have easily skewered any number of Muppets on it before anyone could have stopped him.) Whereas our prehistoric penguin (*Palaeeudyptes klekowskii, named from fossils found in New Zeeland*) was neither cute nor cuddly and sported a pointed beak well over three feet long. In the costume, Clive somehow operated the beak opening so he could time it with the noises he made.

It might help at this point to explain what let Clive overcome his fear of wearing the costume. It had nothing to do with Poirot's failed attempts at hypnosis—in a word, it was pantomime. One day, when Clive joined us at tea, he remarked on how sad it was that he couldn't wear the costume. Poirot and I nodded, absentmindedly reaching for our respective treats, thinking that was the end of Clive's thoughts on the matter. But he went on, recounting how grand he'd felt playing the part of the giant ferocious beast when stomping about at the Tunbridge Wells Commons. He said it felt magnificent and freeing and reminded him of his participation in a play during his King's College days. It had been a children's play he'd been roped into by a drama teacher who stopped him in a hallway with a raised finger pointed at his chest, explaining that she needed someone tall to play a dragon.

"The two have much in common," I said offhandedly. Seeing blank faces, I added, "Dragons? Giant penguins? Monstrous sorts. Quite unlike Clive's reserved demeanor. I mean, no offense, Clive, old son. It's just that maybe you enjoyed the departure. Psychically—in the Freudian sense. Releasing the old id, so to speak?"

"Ah," Poirot said. "So, once in it, he takes on the character. And, as such, as a dragon or giant Kumimanu, he would have no fear."

"That is what I'm getting at," I said.

Clive, for his part, stared into his empty teacup.

"Then the solution is obvious," Poirot said, tapping

his head with a flipper. "We must sneak up on the unsuspecting Clive from behind and jam on the penguin costume head before he can react! Then he will be transformed."

Clive abruptly stood. "You'll do what?"

"Come now, Poirot," I said. "You don't see the problem with that?"

"Ah, my friend, you are right. Neither of us is tall enough to accomplish the deed. Perhaps a step ladder. But that complicates the element of surprise."

"I'm standing right here," Clive said. "I'll have no head jamming."

"Sorry, Clive," I said. "I'm merely pointing out a principle. As you admit, you like being the creature in the suit. So maybe once you get into it, a sort of playfulness might take over, overriding the claustrophobia."

"I did have fun with it while it lasted," Clive admitted. "Maybe I'll give it a go. But," he said, staring at Poirot, "no head jamming."

A few times, on his own, in his flat, without the aid of Poirot or myself, did the trick. After getting over his initial trepidation, he found that once costumed, he enjoyed himself. If anything, he may have been enjoying the role too much. We would assemble in Clive's flat for dress rehearsals with Poirot as director. Arguments over interpretation ensued. Clive felt he correctly embodied the prehistoric creature through acting exercises he'd decided to employ.

With the headpiece off, he was Clive. With the headpiece on, he was the monster penguin.

In this particular session, he had Poirot and me up to his flat to assess various calls he was trying out. These ranged from deep-throated roars to high-pitched shrieks. Sadly, Clive's acting ability left something to be desired, so to spare his feelings, Poirot and I suggested he use something a bit more moderate for the tele or stay silent. I may have made up something about the ancient species lineage being carried on into our modern Mute swan. Though it seemed impractical that any animal would lack some sort of 'hey, look out!' vocalization.

I don't know if you've been to a television studio. I had once when Poirot was on The Report with William Spinacre (a news/entertainment/interview show on BBC1 that runs week nightly.) Because when you have a friend who is less than four feet high, is avian, and lacks opposing thumbs, it's only decent to help them navigate a world made for simians. Upon arrival, Poirot, Clive, and I were escorted to the green room. It was a show with a small live audience—perhaps a hundred—seated in a raised and tiered section behind the cameras, but I chose to stay in the green room and watch it on a monitor in case Clive needed help with his costume. Studios are busy, cluttered places. Central to this one was the set— the one viewed by the television audience—an incongruously homey and inviting scene with a padded chair for the host, an end table to his left, and chairs for guests. Outside that bright oasis, it was dark—a place from which light emitted yet remained unlit—where neither man nor penguin, not part of the crew, was to tread unled.

Spinacre had become enamored with Poirot after the first visit and was amused by Poirot's recitations of his odes to mackerels despite being thinly veiled plagiarisms of Longfellow, Wordsworth, Shelly, Yeats, and other Romantic Era poets. I credit Lady Gilderd Freist-Forstcrindle, talent coordinator for that show (rumored to be Spinacre's paramour), as the one who discovered Poirot as a fine artist and then a popular TV guest.

Currently, as Poirot trumpeted whenever the occasion allowed (or not), we can add *best-selling author* to Poirot's list of accomplishments. His book, *The Lost Antarctic Empire of the Giant Penguins: Bigfoot Solved?* shot to the top of several non-fiction lists. The term *non-fiction*, within the publishing industry, as we know from celebrities' and politicians' autobiographies, is less of an assurance of veracity and more of a bookstore shelving instruction.

We watched on a monitor in the green room. Spinacre's first guest was an actor—Maria Delgado—who was promoting her new movie. This being the Spinacre show—an early evening discussion venue, a bit more serious than the typical late-night yuck-fest—the film was a drama about sisters on opposite sides of the Scottish independence issue. I confess I found her attire, or lack thereof, somewhat distracting. When she started speaking, I was surprised by her Castilian accent—though I should have guessed from her name. There seemed to be a fad in film to cast English or Australian actors as Americans, so I should not have been surprised. After she described the film, I commented to the others in the room that I wondered if the relationship in the film was meant to be a metaphor for difficult family dynamics or if the family dynamics were meant to be a metaphor for the national issue. Poirot did not respond to this as he was pacing back and forth, muttering lines from one of his odes. Which one? I thought I could tell, not from the sotto mutterings, but something about the rhyme of the thing, as Keats—or was it Byron—*She Walks in Beauty in the Night. Da, dum, da, dum, da, dum… (It was Byron, I later confirmed.)*

Clive didn't respond to my metaphorical musings about the film, either. He was busy putting himself into the giant penguin suit.

Soon, there was a commercial break, and with that

came a knock on the door, followed by the door opening. A thin older man wearing a headset on his bald head peered in. I assumed he was the stage manager.

"Mr. Poirot, come with me now." Then, looking askance at Clive, added, "I'll be back for you in five minutes. You will be ready."

I bid Poirot good luck as he went off.

After the commercial break ended, Poirot was shown seated next to Spinacre, and the actress had moved one chair over. I assumed that several minutes of watching Poirot waddle out and clambering into the chair was considered not good TV. Spinacre introduced Poirot and set up a copy of the book resting on the end table next to his chair. The camera zoomed in on the cover as he read out the title.

"Mr. Poirot, it's so good to have you back," Spinacre said. "I wonder—before we get into the book—if you'd grace us with one of your poems. To those who have not heard them, they are wonderful homages to the works of various Romantic poets, with Mr. Poirot's unique spin added."

Watching from the greenroom, I held my breath, wondering if Poirot might take that as an attack on the originality of his odes.

"I would be honored," Poirot said, bowing his head slightly.

I relaxed—he was going to let it slide.

"I must say, however, Mr. Spinacre, these are not simple homage."

I had relaxed too soon.

"No?" Spinacre rejoined. "Not to diminish your work, but you've adapted famous poems to make the subject matter mackerels. I think it's rather clever, and we'd love to hear your latest." He began clapping, hoping to move on, and looked up at the crew, who quickly joined in, as did the guest actress.

"Of course, of course," Poirot said, "I'm flattered, but just to clarify… I see it more as re-framing rather than adaptation—a re-appropriation of what was an anthropomorphic appropriation—not reconceived but conceived as what should have been."

Maria Delgado, the actress, interjected, "If I may. That is not unusual. We Spanish have a literature convention of using an old classic secular poem to make it acceptable as religious by replacing a few words and phrases. We call it *a lo divino*."

"A sort of *a lo penguino*, in this case," Spinacre said. This got a laugh from everyone but Poirot. Spinacre quickly jumped in, "As you say, Mr. Poirot. What do you have for us tonight?"

Seemingly mollified, Poirot stood up in his chair. "I call this *original* work *Night Fishing*." He dramatically waved one flipper and began.

> *"They swim in beauty, like the night*
> *Of cloudless climes and starry skies;*
> *And all best tastes of fins so bright*
> *Meet in the aspect of my eyes;*
> *Thus mellowed by that tender light*
> *Which heaven to gaudy day denies.*
> *One shade the more, or ray the less,*
> *Would half impair their nameless grace*
> *Which waves in every silver tail*
> *Or softly lights up when they race;*
> *Where thoughts serenely sweet avail*
> *How pure, how dear their dwelling place."*

"Wonderful," Spinacre said while politely clapping.

Poirot nodded in acknowledgment, then brushed his forehead as though wiping away the beads of sweat produced by the effort. "I know you understand, but for those watching who may be unfamiliar with a deep understanding of poetic expression, shall I explain a bit—removing the veil, so to say?"

Spinacre nodded. "Oh, please do, Mr. Poirot."

Poirot looked into the camera. "It means some things look better with less light."

"Oh," Spinacre said, adjusting his tie and quickly changing the topic. "We're also here to talk about your book. It looks so exciting," he reached over and touched Poirot's chair. "Your thesis is, I suppose, clear from the title— *The Lost Antarctic Empire of the Giant Penguins*—but I'll let you explain."

"Yes, yes. My book is about our lost history—a history lost in the frozen mists of time. Before a great cataclysm, the penguin species Kumimanu ruled the earth. Then, as science now shows, comet impacts just some twelve-thousand years ago…"

"You say impacts, plural?"

"It could have been one very large comet; everyone was too busy dying to count."

"You're speaking of what they call the Younger Dryas Period, I assume. We've had other guests, recently, promoting that theory, but I think that's still contested."

"Oh, no. Science is in agreement. They gave it a scientific name—the Younger Dryas Period—like the Prehistoric Period or the Bronze Age. Surely, Mr. Spinacre, you're not saying the Bronze Age is in question?"

"I… well, please go on, Mr. Poirot."

"Tragically, that cataclysm wiped out much of life on earth, thus allowing some of the lower species to thrive. The climate changed drastically, and my ancestors' once noble and technologically advanced civilization became— and now remains—buried under miles of Antarctic ice."

"That's quite a claim. I suppose we must wait for Antarctica to melt to verify that."

"As it will. As it will."

"In addition, we have the subtitle of your book: *Bigfoot Solved?* Would you care to explain? I know it must have something to do with the recent *Beast of Tunbridge Wells* incident we all read about. Not to give away the plot, but I understand we have a surprise guest with us tonight."

There was a knock on our green room door, followed by a repeat appearance of the stage manager.

"Time. Follow me."

On the monitor, Poirot was explaining his notion that what people thought of as Bigfoot were, in reality, ancestors of the giant penguins who'd somehow survived and gone feral.

Thankfully, Clive had managed to don the lower part of his suit without my help during the recitation. Only the headpiece remained. It was a bit difficult to manage that last detail using only giant rubber flippers. I picked up the head and told the stage manager I intended to follow close behind and put it on Clive after we wound through the backstage area.

"Fine," he said. "It's a bit dark. Don't you trip."

We turned left, and the lights from the set made the passage seem dim. Clive half-waddled and half-shuffled ahead of me due to the costume's restrictions, which, without the large head, gave him the appearance of a giant bowling pin. We reached a bit of scrim, hiding us from the studio audience, and with the help of the stage manager and Clive awkwardly bending over a bit, I managed to place the penguin head appliance. Clive gave the beak a few openings and closings from the mechanism within, and we were set.

I could hear Spinacre saying, "I understand, Mr. Poirot, that you have a surprise guest for us. The very beast that frightened so many in Tunbridge Wells."

"You're on," the stage manager whispered.

With that, Clive pointed his beak to the sky and let out what was, until then, his most convincing roar. He proceeded onto the set, great rubber flippers waving, his beak gnashing the air, and screeching.

"*Hostia*!" Maria Delgado yelled out. She pulled her feet up on the chair and covered her head.

Spinacre stood, speechless for once, and took a step back. Poirot hopped up and down in his chair, clapping his flippers, seeming pleased. The audience was split between those laughing and applauding and those looking for the exit. Clive proceeded towards Spinacre but, hearing the turmoil from the audience, turned towards the cameras. It appeared to me that, for all intents and purposes, he seemed hell-bent on giving them their money's worth. But then, he proceeded, stepping between the two cameras toward the audience, stopping at a railing that separated the viewers from the set, and began banging on it and roaring. His long beak, thrashing back and forth, caught an elderly man in the face. Nose bleeding, the man yelled out that he'd been bit and held up a bloody hand to prove it—those who'd been laughing flipped into panic mode and headed toward the exits. Clive turned to his right and continued his act, unaware that he'd accidentally injured someone. At some point, despite the reduced visibility from the costume, he must have noticed the panicked exodus because he stopped and started fumbling at his headpiece, eventually removing it and letting it drop to the floor.

"Wait, wait," he yelled. "I'm not a monster!"

I'm not sure how Spinacre's people, the network's people, or whoever's people made things right with those injured in the guest audience. Thankfully, they did not involve Clive or Poirot. Even with my occupation and experience, I'm not sure what a fair compensation might be for a bloody nose derived from an accidental collision with a fake giant penguin beak.

As for Clive, I'm sure he'll stop moping someday and come out of his flat. Until then, I've been enjoying a bit of a reprieve from his overbearing company.

Poirot? Poirot has been living on a cloud. The publicity from the Spinacre show and subsequent social media posts about the disaster shot his book's sales through the stratosphere. But how many more mackerel can one penguin enjoy? No, his true reward was the adoring adulation and appearances at local bookstores. His publishers are pushing for a book tour. Still, he can't travel without assistance, and he's reluctant to use someone assigned by the publisher, as I'd already informed him that I had other business to attend to. But he seems happy enough to bask in more isolated fame. It's not that I have any guilt over not helping him. Not too much, anyway. But I supposed I *could* help him with a limited publicity junket—to Scotland perhaps—no further. While on the topic of guilt, I found myself thinking of Clive, after everything he'd been through, sitting alone in his Aunt's spooky lodgings. Despite the slight cringe it gave me, I resolved to invite him to tea— perhaps tomorrow or the next. Just then, there was a knock at the door. I heard Poirot's bedroom door open, and then the front door, followed by Clive's sheepish, "Hullo, Poirot." I went to the kitchen and started a fresh kettle.

-the end-

# Acknowledgments

Dr. Rebeca Castellanos for reading, editing, and laughing at my jokes, and her partner, the amazing Dr. Médar Serrata, for his encouragement and good humor.

And finally, and most importantly, my patient, beautiful, and wonderful wife, Dr. Judy Whipps.

Please consider these other fine books by this author.

## The Last Border
*(novel, 436 pages, Paperback, Kindle)*

Two years in the aftermath of a Second 9/11—the destruction of Baltimore—a trillion dollars is spent on the border wall with Mexico, yet a ruthless drug cartel magnate, bypasses it with impunity. With the kidnapping of the daughter a US Presidential candidate, Agent Johnny Pinchot of the newly formed Federal Police Service must put aside his distrust and work with Mexico's special agent Oscar Gámez to rescue her while facing the tech-savvy drug lord's far-reaching tentacles of power and influence.

## If I Should Die Before It Wakes, and other stories.
*(collection, 146 pages, Paperback, Kindle, Audio)*

Surprise, humor, and suspense are in these six stories featuring the novelette "If I Should Die Before It Wakes," where a marine biologist discovers a nightmare poised to awaken in the world's oceans.

## Toanan the Heretic
*(novel, 346 pages, Paperback, Kindle, Audio)*

An ancient alien freed from a millennium of mind control by a hunter's stray bullet teams up with a bookish philosopher hired for a secret think tank. The unlikely allies race to save humanity from an other-worldly plot.

## Author's Amazon Page.
https://amzn.to/2AYT5TL

9 798218 803544